I0587873

MAGICIAN RISING

DIVINATION IN DARKNESS BOOK 1

RENÉE DES LAURIERS

For Maya

1

Only twenty minutes left until closing, and some punk kid came rushing through the door, knocking into the discount toothpaste display and scattering boxes on to the floor. Jeff rolled his eyes and got up from his post by the cash register. He didn't get paid enough for this shit.

He'd spent the better part of the afternoon arranging the boxes in neat little rows. Now he had to settle for stacking them back up haphazardly. He'd have to fix it tomorrow before Kevin got on his case about it.

Kevin's Quick & Convenient store had been empty for more than an hour. Of course someone would show up right at the last moment. This kid needed to get out in five minutes for Jeff to close up on time. After his shift, that guy on Craigslist would hold the backup generator for him until nine, but he couldn't press his luck. Someone else would definitely snag it, what with all of the blackouts going around recently. Last time the power went out at the end of the quarter finals of the World Cup, right before France scored the winning goal against Russia. Jeff resorted to googling the scores on his phone and watching recaps on YouTube.

The boy, now pacing up and down through the aisles, was the type that thought it was cool to dress in all black. Pale, and sort of sickly. Jeff didn't like the way the kid's hands were twitching, all shifty-looking. His movements were too jerky to be considered normal. Like he was on drugs or something.

Jeff scowled. If this punk stole something, would he get fired? If it was the wrong thing, maybe. So Jeff stopped at the end of the aisle, straightening cans, just close enough to notice the kid was muttering to himself. Jeff sidled closer.

But that didn't stop the boy from pulling something off the shelf, ripping it open, and eating it right in front of him. Oh, hell no.

"Umm, are you going to pay for that?"

The kid ignored him, jamming another handful into his mouth.

"Hey, kid, I said…" Jeff trailed off. The kid was shoving batteries into his mouth, chomping on them like they were carrot sticks. *What the fuck?*

As he stared, the kid dropped the package of AAs and ripped into another. Chewing and snorting like a pig as he ate.

"Is this some sort of reality TV show?" Jeff looked over his shoulder. "Kevin? Maggie? You can come out now, I'm not buying this. It's not funny. You can stop now."

But no one answered. There was no *hey, you got me*. No hidden camera crew came out and explained what was going on. Just some weird kid making his way through a twenty count package of batteries. Must be drugs then. People did all sorts of crazy things on drugs.

That's it. Jeff didn't like being pushy, but he was going to have to put his foot down. If the boy was high, there was no telling what other crazy stuff he was going to pull. Jeff tapped on his shoulder. "Excuse me, but I'm going to have to ask you to leave."

The kid turned and smiled in a rictus of jagged teeth, ringed with blood. His pupils were constricted into sharp points that didn't meet Jeff's gaze as he crammed the last handful of batteries into his mouth.

Oh, shit.

Time to get out. Or call 911 or something. But if he ditched work, what would happen to his paycheck? Would he even make rent?

The boy smirked at him, the batteries clenched in his grubby fists. Untidy hair, dull brown eyes and what looked like a ketchup stain smeared on his chin. Maybe fifteen years old.

What the hell, wasn't he just... It's late, I need a coffee or something.

"Sir, you're going to have to get out of this store. You are going to have to eat batteries somewhere else."

That seemed to finally get the kid's attention.

"Don't say a word." The boy's words were oddly rhythmic, in his raspy voice. Droplets of red flicked onto his lips as he spoke.

"I'm sorry, but you're defacing company property. I can't let you do that." Jeff wiped his clammy hands on his khakis.

The boy's words continued in an odd sort of croon. "Momma's gonna buy you a Mockingbird."

What did that even mean? "Look, kid, I just caught you shoplifting. Your parents aren't here to buy your mockingbird or whatever."

The kid cocked his head as if straining to hear something. But the store was quiet. It was just the two of them talking, and only one of them was making any sense.

Screw it. Jeff could pay for the damn batteries himself. "Now, I can let you off with a warning, if you promise to leave the store and not come back. There's no need to get the police involved."

It was like a switch flipped. The kid broke into a smile filled with dripping teeth, like a predator baring fangs. "And if that mockingbird don't sing..." He leaned back until his arms touched the metal display shelves.

There was a crack and a bright flash like lightning. Electricity pulsed down the kid's skinny arms to the shelving and into the floor. Above them, the lights flickered spastically on and off. The kid stared for a moment longer and almost seemed to get taller. "Momma's gonna buy you a diamond ring."

The kid turned back to the shelves and grabbed his third fix of AAs.

Let him have all the batteries. This shit was too weird. Jeff tried to take a step away and found that he couldn't.

He looked down at his feet, but he couldn't see them. He tried to pull up his leg, but it was stuck, as if he had stepped into a bucket of cement. Jeff bent down to try yanking at his thigh. His feet and the bottom of his leg disappeared into the floor. It wasn't until he looked back up at the kid that he realized the kid wasn't getting taller. Somehow Jeff was sinking—sinking straight down into the floor.

Jeff looked around for something to hold on to, but the shelves were too far away to reach. He strained toward them anyway as they gradually got further and further out of reach.

"What the hell did you do to me?" Jeff tried to lean forward to reach something and pull himself out, but he was held fast. He kept trying, stretching his shaking hands. Anything to fight against gravity or whatever was pulling him down.

Jeff paused. Someone else was in the store. The new customer was the type of guy who didn't know when to stop going to the gym. Jeff usually had a sense about who was around, but for such a bulky guy, the newcomer was pretty quiet. Didn't even set off the obnoxious chimes at the entrance.

Before Jeff could warn him or even ask for help, the new guy lunged at the battery kid and punched him right in the ribs—at least, Jeff thought it was a punch, until he saw the handle clenched in a white-knuckle grip.

"Momma!" the kid shrieked, high pitched and angry. He thrashed his arms in jerky motions as sparks flew out of his fingertips. The newcomer twisted his fist.

The kid went limp. That was a blade, wasn't it? As it was pulled out, red flowed out onto the floor Jeff had polished three hours before.

The constricted pupils lost their focus as the kid let out a breath like a sigh.

Jeff waited for a moment for the kid to get up. He didn't. The only thing that moved was the dark fluid spreading along the linoleum.

"Did you just kill him?"

The guy turned and kneeled, keeping away from where Jeff's calf should have been, and tapped around the area with the still wet knife. Where his feet sunk below the floor, there was no feeling, as if he had no toes to move at all.

"I might be able to save you." His eyes were pale and piercing, like thin ice over deep water. Jagged pink scars were partially hidden under stubble and light hair, and he frowned as if Jeff's predicament was a particularly challenging sudoku puzzle.

"That sounds great, man." Jeff bit down on his trembling bottom lip.

"You might have a chance if I cut you out from here." He placed the knife against Jeff's upper thigh, close enough to feel the lethal edge of it.

"Woah, woah, woah!" He waved his arms, desperate to push the guy and his knife away. "Stop! Get that thing away from me. You can't chop off my legs! Who the hell do you think you are?"

"Nikolai." His lips pressed together, and his eyes narrowed. "It might be the only way to save your life."

"Save my life? I'm pretty sure that cutting off my legs is a bad idea. A really bad idea. Worse than whatever that psycho kid did to me."

Nikolai sighed. "All right, then." He wiped his blade on the kid's shirt and started walking back down the aisle. He disappeared around the shelves.

"Wait, where are you going? Can't you at least call for help or something? You can't just leave me here!"

Nikolai said nothing, but he did return a moment later with a fire extinguisher in hand.

"How's that going to help?"

Nikolai swung the extinguisher down to the floor, smashing the tiles and cracking the cement below. Over and over, in a way that would almost certainly get Jeff fired.

Jeff looked at all those jagged edges of broken cement. Shouldn't that have hurt?

Why couldn't he feel those little rocks that went flying?

Nikolai dug out chunks of cement, tossing them off to the side. He stopped and cursed, dropping the extinguisher with a clank.

"What is it?"

"The parts of you that went under are just gone."

"What do you mean gone? Can't you try pulling me out?"

Nikolai shook his head. "I tried that on the last guy. It didn't work."

Jeff swallowed. The floor was almost to his hips and showed no signs of stopping. "Please, there has to be something." He shut his eyes, nausea pooling in the pit of his stomach. "My legs. You can cut them."

"It's too late for that. I'm sorry."

Jeff looked for reprieve in Nikolai's stoic expression and found nothing.

Jeff was actually disappointed to hear that it was too late to cut off body parts.

"Could you leave me alone for a minute?" The chatter in his teeth was agonizingly audible. There was no pretending to be brave.

"If it starts to become painful," Nikolai said, "I can end things quickly for you."

"Okay, Jesus, just give me a second."

"I'll be by the door if you change your mind."

Jeff pulled his phone from his pocket, looking away when he noticed the floor looming right below.

On his lock screen, there she was—his golden-haired beauty. What was going to happen to her? The last words of the kid brought Jeff inspiration. He flipped through to his favorites and pressed call. It went to voicemail. Jeff hung up and called again. He listened to it ring, muttering, "Come on, the one day I need you to pick up, come on."

"Hello?"

"Hey!" Jeff bent his arms higher, stretching up at an awkward angle as high as he could go. He tried to sound normal, chipper even, but his throat was tight, his voice a strung bow.

"Jeff? What is it, are you okay?"

"Something happened today at work. Mom, I need to ask you something." He was eye level with the laundry detergent on the bottom shelf. He refused to look down.

"Did you go off on a customer or something?"

"Not like that. Look, I need you to take care of Roxie for me." The bottom of his elbow was stuck in place, holding the phone to his ear.

"What, you don't call in two weeks and then ask me to watch your dog?"

Jeff took a ragged breath. "Just promise me."

"All right, fine."

He'd only taken her for a short walk that morning. He'd promised her a longer one, just as soon as he got back. By now she'd be waiting at the front door for him, nose tucked between her little paws. Wagging her stubby tail at any noise approaching the door. Wondering why he never came home. "Just don't forget to put the cheese on top of her kibble, and don't let her eat alone. She won't eat if she's left alone."

"I know." She let out a deep sigh. "I still have the instructions from last time. All six pages."

He could see the floor sucking him in, like sinking down into ocean waves. "I'm sorry about Thanksgiving. It was stupid of me, and you shouldn't have to put up with that. I lo—" He suddenly couldn't move his lips anymore. He couldn't feel his mouth.

"It's okay. I love you, too."

The floor was up to his nose, and then he couldn't breathe.

No, no, no. This couldn't be happening. He was just four

online classes away from finishing his degree and finally being able to quit this place. He'd made reservations for that fancy new restaurant, and he was going to do it. He was finally going to ask Jamie from the dog park out on a date. He was going to...

The floor was up to his eyes, a wall of linoleum as far as he could see. Then everything went black.

Jun stared at the fortune cookie with more suspicion than a confection made of flour, sugar, and vanilla extract normally deserved. There was no way a cookie could have any impact on her destiny—the little strip of paper inside was entirely useless. So why did she make no move to toss it into the bowl smeared with Moo Goo Gai Pan sauce and be done with it? She grabbed it and found herself snapping it open instead and muttered the message. "Change not what you carry, but what you carry it with."

Stupid. Jun shook her head. Why did she even bother? The leftovers of her rushed meal went into the trash. Her shift was just about to start.

Jun shuffled her uniform cap in her hands. She still had five minutes, and the Campus Shop was right there.

In the display window beneath the 50% off sign was the Fenty mascot bag she'd been eyeing for weeks—special edition in her school's colors and in the classic teddy bear shape. Bear. Like the school mascot. Like her last name. The plush chenille fabric called to her.

Don't even think about it.

Bad luck courted Jun like a lover, and she didn't want to give any signs that she believed in their relationship. Besides, her backpack was fine. Sure, she had gotten it in high school and the fabric was wearing down, but she had more important things to worry about.

Jun waited until she entered Feelin' Saucy before jamming on a cap featuring a smiling pizza slice.

"Hey, Antonio. What do you got for me?" Jun unhooked the keys behind the counter. The plastic epitaph chained to it declared that *pizza is the only love triangle I want.*

She cringed at the pizza boxes stacked to half her height. Her shift was supposed to be over before her next class.

It was okay. There was still enough time.

Antonio patted the top of the stack like it was an obedient pet. "You know what to do."

"Thanks, man." Jun scooped up the boxes, leaning so that they wouldn't hit her in the face. She maneuvered out of the back door and into the Crust Mobile, a van with the tacky drawing of a pizza on the door panels and mesh wire along the side windows. It was a fitting name. Every day on the job, without fail, she'd found pieces of crust in the seams of the seat. She loaded the pizzas into the hotbox and was off campus before the long hand made its way once around the clock.

"All right, first order, two-sixty-two Shattuck Ave." A light drizzle coated the windows. The sky was a dreary gray that promised a storm. She started up the Crust, calculated the quickest route, then was on the road. The windshield wipers smeared the rain into wet streaks.

Noticing college-aged guys on the sidewalk, Jun pulled the cap low on her forehead and slouched in her seat. They probably weren't in her class. Even if they were, they wouldn't recognize Jun in her uniform. Probably.

Jun flipped on the radio, shifting between the three stations that worked. She switched it from the one station that was half light jazz, half loud static. The next station played the news, something about a reward for any leads into the disappearance of a Jeff Thompson—well, that was depressing. The third station was probably music, but no matter what time her shift was, it always played commercials. Jun let a soothing voice explain why she should hurry in today, because there was no way this discount flooring deal could last.

Ignoring the main roads, with their line of cars all bumper to bumper for as far as the eye could see, she instead went down the little streets hugged by cheerful suburban houses. Her meandering path was only seven minutes faster than sitting in traffic, but it was worth it. California drivers reacted to drizzle like it was the apocalypse.

It only took her so far before she was forced back to the main roads. She merged neatly, matching the flow of the other cars on the road. Neither of these things stopped the car in the left lane from drifting over her way.

What the hell? He wasn't even signaling. Jun honked the horn and the Crust let out a squeaky low whine, just in time for the guy to swerve wildly back into his own lane. He squinted his eyes darkly, getting a good look at her.

The guy lined his Camry next to her at the red light, ignoring ten feet of space in front of him. He lowered his windows and started ranting about her "stupid ass" and the murderous, life-ending qualities of "Asian women." Well, Jun wasn't even full Japanese, so at most the words could only be half true.

She bopped her head to a laundry detergent jingle. It wasn't bad, actually. Kind of catchy. Maybe it was right.

Maybe lavender fabric softener was the thing that was missing from her life.

"Hey!" The guy got out of his car and started pounding against the door of the Crust Mobile.

She forced a bored expression onto her face, even as she tightened her grip on the steering wheel so that he wouldn't see her fingers trembling.

"Get off the road and go back to your country, you stupid bitch!" He flipped her off with both hands before stepping back into his car. He still didn't move forward though, just kept his car nearby so that he could glare at her.

This red light couldn't last any longer.

Was he trying to watch her go back to her native soil? Jun was born forty miles from here.

The car sped off as soon as the light flipped to green.

Jun reached into her pocket to run her fingers around her knitted merino wool keychain. She took a deep breath and turned up the radio to block out the bleating honks behind her.

She was fine. Her face in the rear-view mirror was only a tad pale.

Two blocks and a quick parallel park later, Jun and her box of pizza got buzzed into an apartment complex. A sweaty guy answered her knock. While counting the pizza money out, deliberate and slow, he stared blatantly at her chest.

"Juun?" The guy tried to read her name tag with a stuttering *uhhh* in the middle.

"It's pronounced Jun. Like the month in summer."

He seemed to take this as an invitation for more. It wasn't. "Pretty name for a pretty little thing." He thought he was being charming as he smiled too widely and handed her the cash. Though the paper was moist, Jun acted like it wasn't.

"That didn't include tip," Jun replied, adding it up quickly.

"I'll give you a ten-dollar tip if you can help me feel saucy," he said with an unwanted wink, eyes fixed firmly on her chest.

God, she didn't get paid enough for this.

Not all of her deliveries were this gross. She hadn't known that Feelin' Saucy had a certain reputation before she got hired. Some of her customers had expectations that Jun did not sign up for. If it weren't for the food discount, she would have been out the door already.

"Err... Thanks. I'll take that under advisement." Jun was already backing away. Thankfully, he got the hint. Halfway down the hallway, she whispered to herself. "From now on, Mr. Shattuck Ave, your orders are going to the bottom of the pile."

The rest of her deliveries went by smoothly without any further harassment, and Jun dropped off the Crust with enough time to make it to her night class. The second she was out the door, she stuffed her work cap into her backpack and replaced it with her knitted hat. Rushing, she threw a jacket over the primary red and blue of the Feelin' Saucy uniform and zipped it up to keep her work history secret. Normally she would change, but this would have to do.

The rain made her jacket stick to her skin, but the Business Analytics room wasn't far. Just a quick walk and she'd be inside. Jun shifted her backpack to a more comfortable position—there was some notebook, pressed at an odd angle. Just a quick tug should fix it. She heard the rip in the middle of the crosswalk, but before she could do anything about it, the strap snapped. Everything spilled out onto the wet pavement.

She snatched up her crochet needles and yarn first, now covered in muck. Her knitting project was ruined. Reflected in the puddles was an orange flash, warning her that the street signal was about to change with her in the middle of it.

Where was her cap? Of course that stayed in the bag. She pulled it all into her arms in an awkward hug. That looked like everything. She got it all, right? She looked back behind her.

"No!" Jun noticed the essay she had stayed up until three in the morning finishing just before the signals changed and the line of cars charged over it.

Jun stuffed everything into the backpack the best she could and held it all by one strap in the crook of her arm. She stood on the curb, fingernails between her teeth, waiting for the light to change back.

It was too late. The papers were mush, not even solid enough for her to pick up. There was no way to tell that this had even been computer paper at one point. She couldn't turn this in. Class was starting in five minutes and it would take twice that to get to her dorm and print this out again.

Jun swung her backpack behind her awkwardly on one strap and ran. She was panting when she threw open her dorm door. Her roommate was hunched over Jun's last piece of cheesecake, fork halfway to her mouth.

So that's why her food disappeared. Jun had her suspicions, but now she knew.

Suzie scowled, continuing on with her bite. Her eyes were narrowed in a way that was surely intended to be menacing, but instead made her look like she was squinting.

Jun's dad had bought that cake special for her from

Fournée's. She was saving it for later today as a treat for turning in her midterm essay.

"What the hell are you doing here?" Suzie said between chewing creamy perfection into oblivion.

"Umm, you see, I live here. At least on that side." Jun gestured over to the tidy section of the room, decorated with her knitted blankets and crocheted ornaments.

"Don't you have class?" Another bite of cheesecake disappeared forever.

Jun pointed to the last bit of dulce de leche caramel cheesecake topped with almonds and mousse on a vanilla crust. "That was mine."

"Like your broke self could afford something like this." Suzie rolled her eyes and took another bite.

"Have you been stealing my food?"

The fork clattered down against the plate as Suzie got up to her feet. She scraped the chair against the floor and got right into Jun's space. "Aren't you here on some kind of merit scholarship? If my aunt on the board heard about all your fake accusations, it wouldn't look so good for you. Maybe you should watch yourself." Suzie smirked, though the effect was ruined by the smudge of cake stuck to her lip.

"I don't have time for this." Jun rushed to the computer, praising all that was good in the world that at least it was still logged in. She clicked on BAmidterm_3rd_edition, and pressed print. The seven pages she agonized over came back into the world. The clicking and swishing sounds of the printer almost blocked out the loud chewing.

As the last page churned out, Jun stapled it neatly and made a silent promise that she would be better, try harder, and do everything different if she could move fast and get there without anything else going wrong.

The rain was heavier on the way back. She hadn't

thought about needing an umbrella, and now she was drenched. Jun clutched her bag under her jacket. She wouldn't let anything happen to her paper again.

When she stumbled through the doors into the classroom, she found it empty. It was just ten minutes after the start, and there wasn't a single person in sight.

"No!" Jun exclaimed to the empty room. "No, no, no, no... I can't believe this." She pressed her face into her palm and thought hard. Professor Cartwright must have collected the midterm finals and sent the class home. But his office was one floor up, through a maze of hallways. Jun didn't even try to make it look like she wasn't sprinting. She ignored the startled expressions of the people she passed in the hallways, not slowing down until she made it to his door.

She knocked sharply.

It opened partway. All she could see was his wrinkled face frowning down at her.

"Professor Cartwright, my essay." Jun thrust the paper toward him.

The professor shook his head. "This is late."

Her jaw dropped open.

Cartwright opened the door wider to scowl at her properly. "My syllabus clearly states that late work is not acceptable under any circumstances."

He moved to shut the door, but couldn't as Jun's dripping sneaker was jammed in the way.

"Your syllabus defines late as over fifteen minutes. It's only eight-fourteen now." She held her essay firm enough to hide the tremble in her hands. She didn't break eye contact with him.

"Very well." The professor sniffed as he took Jun's midterm.

Jun closed her eyes and breathed a sigh of relief.

"But the standard forty percent penalty applies."

Heat flushed to her cheeks; her heart was pounding. This couldn't be happening.

"Sir, you don't understand. The paper was finished on time, but I dropped it and it got run over by a car. I had to reprint it and I got here as fast as I could," Jun rambled. She was seeing bright spots; the edges of her vision were blurring. Just what she needed was to start crying right now.

"There's always going to be a reason why things are late. That doesn't make it acceptable. In the words of Benjamin Franklin, 'You may delay, but time will not.'"

"But, sir." The professor hadn't heard her. The wrinkled arm disappeared into his office, taking her essay away with it.

Jun turned, staring blankly at the wall, taking deep breaths. She would have turned to knitting to calm herself if it wasn't all the way back at her dorm, covered in mud.

It wasn't fair. Could she do anything about it? How much damage would this do to her GPA?

She did a quick mental calculation—it was enough to drop her grades below the minimum she needed to maintain. What would happen if she lost her scholarship? Her father would want to help of course, but how could she let him? She had whittled away at his retirement funds enough already.

Jun tried to take a step away, but she felt heavy. A headache flashed brilliant, pounding and aching in the back of her head.

"This day needs to be over already," Jun groaned. "It can't get any worse. It can't."

And that was when the earthquake started—a tremor below her feet.

Her heart dropped, exactly as it had the one and only time she went on a rollercoaster. The shaking got worse. She reached for a wall, and unable to keep a steady balance, she slid down. There was nothing to hide under. Wasn't that what she was supposed to do? Hide under something? She lifted her bag over her head.

A sharp cracking noise split through the air. The rumbling continued as if it would break through the floor. Something heavy fell. The tiles around her cracked, and Jun realized how foolish it was to stay here. But once she crawled to her feet, trailing her hands along the walls, the tremors slowed, stopping completely at her first step away.

Jun stood some moments, shakily, with a strange buzz in her ears. Someone faraway yelled. There was always the possibility that part of the building could collapse. They would have to evacuate. Professor Cartwright, she realized, was still in his office and might need assistance.

An ear-splitting wail went through the halls as the fire alarm sounded. Jun went over to the door and pushed it, as there was some resistance. "Professor?" Jun had half the door open. "Are you..." Her words fell away at the sight of the hole taking up nearly half the office floor. It was impossible to look without risking following him down.

"Oh, God." She backed away from the room. "Someone help!"

Her words were swallowed by the alarm. Some faculty members and students scrambled for the stairs, while a few other were barking orders, trying to be heard over the alarms. When she tried to get help, no one could hear her and Jun went down the flight of stairs, hoping that someone below was already assisting her professor.

There were people there, a small crowd gathering in the room directly below her professor's as fellow students ignored the shouts to vacate the building. Some were taking pictures, and even filming it on their phones. Jun went closer. She was nearly elbowed in the face by an older senior, and her hat was knocked off and stepped on. When she bent to pick it up—more wary now of the much bigger bodies—she saw through their legs the collapsed desk and Dr. Cartwright sprawled atop of it. His elderly body seemed to be bent at an unnatural angle.

Other students were being forced to leave, and Jun jumped back before they could step on her. She went with the others outside. The blare of the fire trucks' sirens and lights hurtled through the night streets. Other students were pointing up. A bright light behind the scattered rain clouds seemed to glow iridescently above them. It was the moon. Except the moon was already an accountable crescent in the other end of the sky.

Her fingers hadn't stopped trembling. She gripped her knitted keychain.

None of it made any sense.

3

The Uber dropped Nikolai off in front of a multi-use apartment in a commercial shopping plaza. The stores were generic enough—UPS, laundromat, nail salon. There was a bagel shop that could be problematic, judging by the amount of foot traffic it was attracting. Otherwise the location was discreet. Clear lines of sight without foliage obstructing the view. It would do.

He rang the cracked doorbell for 1306 Durant Ave and listened to the thud of heavy feet moving downstairs. A man with hooded eyes and a tribal tattoo peeking out along his collarbone answered. He moved aside, allowing Nikolai in.

The apartment was bare, save for an old sofa, a card table with folding chairs, and the lingering smell of paint. Leaning against the tile countertop of the combined kitchen and living space was a man that Nikolai had never met, though he had heard of him.

"So you're it, then?" He was an older man for this line of work—his curly red hair was graying at the temples. Nevertheless, his reputation preceded him. Roman Walker. His team took out the Florida fire-eater about two years back. "I asked for someone experienced. How many have you taken out?"

Was this guy serious? "Do you mean in total, or just this year?" Roman didn't respond, just waited for an answer. "Forty-three. Last one was causing all those power outages."

"Oh, that was you, was it? Heard that one was a nasty piece of work. How did you do it?"

In response, Nikolai flicked out a blade from a panel hidden in his sleeve.

Meteorite iron dampened most magic. Some in the business had modern creations, but these had been in Nikolai's family for generations.

Roman leaned closer in interest. "I've seen knives like that once before. You wouldn't happen to be related to Mikhail Vasiliev?"

"He was my brother." Nikolai sheathed the blade.

Roman nodded, as if he was considering him and didn't find Nikolai lacking. "What with housing costs being what they are around here, we could only get a three bedroom. I've got the master. Pistachio—he's registering us with the college right now. He's got seniority. That leaves you and David here." Roman nodded toward the man with the shoulder tattoo who was following the conversation with interest. "You two could fight for the room. First drawn blood is the winner. Nothing incapacitating, of course."

Nikolai didn't come here to play games. "You can have the room. It doesn't matter to me." He threw his suitcase on the old sofa. As the bag thudded against scratched sofa leather, David stopped right in the middle of cracking his knuckles.

Though the earthquake was over a week ago, Nikolai might find clues yet. "I'm going out. Text me if you need me."

Nikolai dressed for the hunt. Everything was strategically nondescript—clothes with no logos, neutral colors. Nothing that would stand out and make him noticeable. Wearing all black was asking for trouble. Might as well throw on a ski mask and gun and tell the world that you're out to rob a gas station.

He worked out which building it was from the corner of a picture from a newspaper article. It was only three letters and a bit of scaffolding, but it was enough. The caution tape at the front doors weren't exactly subtle either. The area was blocked off and filled with construction workers.

Nikolai was forced to wait on a bench under the shade of a redwood preserved from the original forest that stood here before the school. The afternoon sun faded, and the light muted into gray.

He tried to guess at the level of repairs from all the loud hammering, trying not to imagine what they could be doing with the evidence. Hunks of concrete and garbage bags were loaded on a dump truck. He noted the license plate in case he had to follow the truck later. Spending the night going through rubble wasn't ideal, but he would do it if it meant finding a lead.

As the last of the construction workers stepped out and the dump truck drove away, Nikolai sidled up to the lock on the door. It was a common pin tumbler lock. His tension wrench and pick unlocked it as smoothly as if he had a key. He slipped his tools neatly back into his pocket and stepped inside.

The lights in the hallway were motion sensor activated and switched on as he walked, flooding the surrounding area with a dull fluorescence. The hallway was oddly pristine. Through the door's glass panel, everything in the classroom was in order. Chairs and desks were lined in straight rows. The podium was upright at the front of the room. The other rooms were much the same. If he hadn't personally watched the construction crew haul things out, he would've sworn he was in the wrong place. He pushed through the hallway doors, and the normal scene slid away.

The cracks started on the stairway, leading up to the second floor where they spiderwebbed across the wall in thin lines. Nikolai held his finger just up to the edge of one of the lines, short of touching it, and followed the thickening mark of damage around the bend until he got to a door that was sealed off with caution tape and locked. Curious. Nikolai unlocked it and slid underneath the yellow plastic. Inside the room, there was a gaping hole like the mouth into hell. It tore through the bottom of the floor, and hunks of concrete remained littered across the room below. Nikolai could see straight down into a lecture hall.

The smell in the room was faint but unmistakable. Clean, like ozone and chlorine, but slightly burned. Magic. Powerful magic at that, if the smell of it lingered for a week.

Not much remained in the room, except a desk piled with papers and a framed newspaper article. Nikolai picked up an essay at the top, and read *Jun Bear, Professor Cartwright, Business Analytics Midterm Final.* He skimmed through the writing.

As far as segmentation strategies, the business targets middle income groups through promoting products that the customer perceives as more upscale and "trendy."

He would hazard a guess that he wasn't about to find anything magic here, but he took the entire stack regardless.

Professor Cartwright. Currently in intensive care, according to the campus newsletter. The sole victim of the earthquake.

The damage was localized to this room. The caved in

ceiling matched the destruction Nikolai would expect from a 6.5 magnitude earthquake. Strong, but less than what he'd expect from the scent left behind. Let alone the earthquake lights that alerted a team of hunters.

No. This seemed personal.

Nikolai looked into the pit that ripped apart the professor's room.

Whoever had done this seemed capable of worse.

His phone rang.

"You lost or something?" Roman's dulcet tones echoed over the cellphone.

"Or something." Nikolai paid Roman half a mind, scanning over the room for any clues he might have missed.

"We're picking classes to check tomorrow. You have any preference? There's Economics, Finance and Marketing, Business Analytics, a computer science class…"

"Yeah, Professor Cartwright's classes," Nikolai stated, while looking down into the mangled remnants of the lecture hall below.

"I can give you one of his. David and Pistachio were thinking the same."

Nikolai checked the stack of paper in his hands. "Business Analytics, then."

THURSDAY AT 8:15 P.M., SITTING IN THE BACK ROW OF THE Business Analytics class, Nikolai observed Cartwright's students. None looked like a magician. Some of them wore collared shirts and ties, typing notes on laptops.

Who goes to class in a tie?

He thought his gray sweats and shirt with the school's

bear mascot would have allowed him to blend in, but that wasn't the case.

Most of the conversations were about the professor. He was still in critical condition. There wasn't a single nice thing said about Mr. Cartwright—in fact, the words 'deserved it' popped up at least three times. Nikolai took special notice of those who held a grudge against the man.

As an older man stepped inside hesitantly, wearing a stiff suit with sharp creases, the chatter spiked.

"Settle down, settle down. Class is in session." His voice was about as engaging as a sack of potatoes. "I'll be covering for Professor Cartwright." He then wrote his name on the whiteboard. *Dr. Goldstein.*

"When will Professor Cartwright return?"

"At this moment his recovery time hasn't been specified—"

"Do we still have to wear these ties?" someone in the front interrupted.

Goldstein looked down at the papers in his hand. "Ah, concerning Dr. Cartwright's syllabus, if you wish to continue to receive extra credit then yes, wear the tie. Now, roll call." He adjusted his glasses as he peered down at the papers. "Rick Abbot." One hand went up from a scrawny kid in the front of the room.

"Bailey Allen." Another hand.

"Tom Bates."

"Here."

"Jon Bear."

"It's Jun," called out the girl who was the only other person sitting in the back row. Nikolai must have overlooked her the first time around. That, or she came in late. She wore a purple hat and hid yarn and needles under her desk and was currently knitting without looking down.

"Ah, yes." The professor scribbled something in the margins. "Evan Campbell?" A new hand was raised. "Louis Cooper."

Nikolai wrote down all their names and circled the ones who looked promising. Jotting down hair color, approximate weight, watching them out of the corner of his eyes.

Goldstein fiddled with his projector. "As I understand, you left off on chapter eight in your books: ideas that shaped the business world."

Nikolai tuned out the talk of stakeholders and allocations, instead looking for twitching fingers, tapping, quick angular movements. Many magicians didn't have the control to hide the natural response of their body to the electric call of magic. He'd heard it described like a high, similar to a hit of heroin once they were properly addicted.

If there was anything to see, the magician hid it well. But if there was a magician in this school, chances were he was hiding in this very room.

4

The phone's persistent buzz startled Jun awake, and she reached out from her heavy Merino wool covers just a moment too late. She greeted the missed call with a raspy "hello," and squinted against the bright screen light instead. Four missed calls. Three missed texts—all from her father.

Jun jolted up in her bed. Her dad must be panicked by now; she had to call him back.

Jun hadn't called him on the night of the earthquake. Why worry him? He must have seen the email the school sent out with the new earthquake evacuation plans, with the headline "Business Professor Hospitalized." It was just too much to hope that he wouldn't check his email this time. The phone didn't get to ring twice.

"Jun! Are you okay? What's this about an earthquake?"

"It was just a small one." Jun smiled as she held the phone to her ear to make her voice sound cheerful. "Most of us barely even noticed it."

"ABC-Seven made it sound more serious than that."

Jun couldn't help wincing at the panic in his voice, how

he was practically gasping for breath. Natural disasters raging across his only child's college campus were just about the last thing he needed to hear about. "It was probably just a slow news day. It was either this or the latest rescue dog adopted into the police force."

"Wasn't it your teacher who got hurt? Didn't he end up in the hospital?"

Jun swallowed hard. The last time she saw him, Professor Cartwright's body was broken across the floor, his mouth agape, his eyes unfocused. Latest gossip was that he was still in intensive care, and it wasn't clear whether or not he was going to make it.

Jun kept her voice light. "Cartwright was practically ancient. The wind could have just as easily knocked him over. The news is blowing this out of proportion. It's nothing to worry about."

The line at the other end of the call went quiet as her father digested this new information. Then he sighed. "I do worry, though. You're working too hard." He spoke slowly, as if there was a tired pause lingering after each word.

"Just keeping busy. I'm fine, Dad."

The TV across the room turned on. The volume increased until the *Bachelor* rerun was cringingly loud. Suzie glared at the screen, remote in hand, refusing to make eye contact when Jun mouthed, "One more minute."

Jun tugged off the glorious warmth of her blankets and tucked her feet into fuzzy pink slippers, then stepped outside to finish her call. The moment she was out, Suzie slammed the door shut behind her.

If housing wasn't such a major impact on Jun's financial aid eligibility, she'd just move back in with her dad.

"What was that?" her father asked when she could finally hear him again.

"Just some party going on downstairs."

"You still on for The Sushi Blanket?"

"Wouldn't miss it for anything," Jun said, not having to force a smile for once.

"Love you, Jun Berry."

"Yeah, see you soon."

If only pretending that everything was okay could make it so. The illusion of normality was shattered as Jun returned to her Business Analytics class. They moved across campus into an old auditorium, a disused science building with curved tiered tables in rows. Fifteen minutes before class started, Jun arrived and sat in the back. She sighed in relief and took out her yarn, letting one finger twist into a coil of soft Cheviot. Okay, no earthquake. So far so good.

Soon others began to stream in, and for a second Jun worried that she might have the wrong place. Gone were the ties and collared shirts. They arrived, flip-flops slapping against tiles and legs bare from the knees. Clean shaven faces were replaced with five o'clock shadows.

Then he came in.

He might have been wearing a simple grizzly hoodie and jeans, but even that loose material wasn't enough to hide lines of muscle. Everything about the man was hard, from his close-cropped hair, to the angle of his jaw, to his stare as his eyes swept across her classmates.

He was not in their cohort. After three years sharing classes, she thought that someone else would notice that this guy appeared out of nowhere. In their last class, she assumed that one of the football players simply wandered into the wrong room, what with classes shifted about for the earthquake repairs last week.

He had been vigilantly focused, but at all the wrong times. While everyone else was jotting down definitions, he was watching the other students. Not once did he look at the professor. She was willing to bet his notes had nothing to do with stakeholder requirements.

Why was he here again?

He walked down the aisles with the confidence of someone who belonged, and Jun forced herself to look away as he came nearer, straight into her row and toward her. He stopped just four seats away.

Jun's mouth went dry.

She fought to silence the feeling that there was something not right about the man; something feral.

Her hands started to shake. She grasped her yarn tight and started a new row. She let the familiar motion of wool rocking back and forth, the needles nothing more than an extension of her fingers, calm her. Just enough to take away the worst sting of anxiety. Holding it at bay, until it was nothing more than a prickle at the back of her neck. She could handle this.

She surrendered herself to the rhythm of the weaving, letting the sense of danger fade to a whisper.

From four seats away, it was obvious he wasn't paying attention to the lecture. But it wasn't until the class was over, and everyone was packing up their stuff, and their substitute made a quick retreat that things got weirder.

"Hey, did anyone hear if Cartwright died yet?" Evan said a little too loudly to his friends.

Jun winced. Well, she got it. Cartwright used Evan's last essay as an example of what not to do, but was that reason enough to wish him dead?

He got a couple groans and a few nasty snickers for that. In front of her, Bailey muttered, "That's such a dick thing to say." But the unwelcome guest looked right at Evan and then flicked back to his notebook. It was angled so that she could just read *Evan: asked about Cartwright's death* out of the corner of her eye before he snapped the notebook shut.

Jun slipped quietly out the back after that. She didn't want any part of whatever that notebook meant. It was already dark, the air unusually foggy, when she crossed campus for Feelin' Saucy.

A stack of boxes was waiting for her. Alexa was at the register, texting on her phone, and Jun walked around her to pick up the boxes.

"Hey," Jun called out as she reached under the counter for the key.

Alexa nodded in reply, not taking her eyes off the screen. Her coworker cut her uniform low enough to catch a glimpse of the black lace of her bra and tied the bottom of her shirt into a knot, revealing the pink glint of a belly ring. She'd just started last week.

Jun maneuvered herself out to the Crust Mobile, juggling the cardboard boxes just enough to unlock it. She skimmed through the address list, noting her regulars. Jun rolled her eyes when she saw Shattuck Ave. As promised, Jun reorganized the stack to deliver that pizza last.

She'd quit if she had any luck finding a better job—or any luck with jobs in general. Her last job was cult affiliated, and the one before that the manager "forgot" to pay her for three weeks.

She kept to the speed limit through the fog, sticking to quiet backroads as she cut her path across the gloom. Her first address was new, but she recognized the location, smack dab in the middle of El Cerrito Plaza. It was a common off-campus housing location, and Jun mentally crossed her fingers that she wouldn't see anyone she knew.

She parallel parked in front of a sleek luxury apartment complex, one of the newly built ones that cost four times as much as Jun's dorm room. As she was buzzed through the gate, she passed cultivated palm trees and the rectangle of a backlit swimming pool.

Her elevator alerted her in a cheerful feminine tone when she arrived at the fourth floor. Her steps faltered—this place was fancy. The corridor was chrome trimmed with room numbers engraved in crystal plaques. Jun pulled her work cap low, shielding as much of her face as possible, just before pressing the doorbell.

As soon as the door opened, she bit her lip when she recognized that profile, the shape of his head, having spent the better part of two years sitting behind him—it was Bailey. She looked at the pizza box, hoping that breaking eye contact would stop him from recognizing her in turn.

"Hey, Jun! What are you doing here?"

Shit.

"Uh..." There really wasn't any way to save this. "I got your order."

He then looked down at the large square box between them. "Oh, of course. I had no idea that you worked for the Sauce." Bailey opened the door a little wider as he leaned against the frame. "They are the best pizza in town," he said with an amiable grin. It was obvious he had recently returned from either a swim or a shower, refreshed, while Jun was positive that the aroma of pizza had imbued into her clothes. She always felt grimy while in her uniform.

"Yeah, the pizza is great. Fresh ingredients and all that." Jun kept her voice normal as she died a little on the inside. Though it wasn't bad, Jun knew for a fact that the majority of guys that ordered from Feelin' Saucy didn't just have pizza in mind. Not that there was anything wrong with some harmless flirting, but her classmates were different. And Bailey always treated her like a professional, just like another one of the guys. He was actually one of her go-to guys for group assignments. How could she talk economics with him now?

Which was why, as he looked her over, it made Jun uncomfortably aware that her uniform was unnecessarily tight. She normally wore a small, but this ridiculous shirt was practically a child's size.

"Hey, what are you doing after this?"

"Probably working on that variance analysis essay." She pushed the box forward, hoping he'd take the hint.

"That's a shame." He stepped back inside for his wallet, affording Jun with a view of a sleek, modern apartment. A huge gray cat watched her lazily from a couch before abruptly licking its hind leg. From another room, a TV was playing a commercial about life insurance. Bailey returned with a few bills. "I'll catch you some other time, then." He gave her a wink.

Jun was halfway down the hall when she realized that her twenty-dollar tip had his number written on it. She shook her head.

He was kind of cute, and she sort of liked him, but if she wanted it to stay that way, a date was off the table. Her luck with dating was especially bad. Her last boyfriend hadn't even lasted a full day before his clothes somehow caught fire when he was making toast.

Graduation was right around the corner. She could deal with heartbreak and emotional fall-out then. When was the last time she even went on a date? Had it really been over a year since Andrew? She didn't want to think about it.

She dropped off pizza for three regulars before she got to another new address. Durant Avenue was another popular off-campus housing spot, but what were the chances that she bumped into two people she knew from school on the job? She parked in front of a cute little shopping complex. There was a family run bagel shop that Jun knew from experience served the good stuff, as well as a laundromat. Perched on the second floor were apartment buildings.

With four boxes of pizza, she went through the doorway, realized that the laundromat had no stairwell leading upstairs, and crushed a corner of the cardboard when she hastily backtracked. Only two little old ladies even bothered to look up briefly from folding laundry. Okay, she spotted the entrance on the other side of the laundromat. A green door with chipped paint was marked with 1306.

Jun was lifting the corner of the first box, making sure that none of the cheese was stuck to the edges or the crust ripped, so when the door opened, the first thing she saw was his bare arms. Jagged lines of scar tissue, some white and faded, others just scabbing over, ran down his arms in angry patterns.

She recognized those arms. Had sat just a few seats away from them.

"There you are," he said.

She caught his eye, pale and fierce—the stranger intruding on her class.

When he grabbed the boxes, Jun saw that his knuckles were bruised. "Took you long enough," he muttered under his breath. "So you got the meat lovers, pepperoni, mushroom, and the one with artichokes and olives and shit."

"Yeah, all here," Jun said.

He had two twenty-dollar bills and a ten ready.

She swallowed past the growing anxiety. "That'll be fifty-eight dollars and seventy cents please."

"Assholes didn't give me enough." He balanced the boxes in one arm, reaching for his wallet in his back pocket. With more dexterity than she'd expected, he took out another twenty-dollar bill. "Here." The money dropped into her hand.

"Nikolai!" yelled a voice from up the stairs. The stranger looked up at the sound of his name. "Stop flirting with the pizza guy, we're starving up here!"

His arms tensed, and he scowled. He turned back inside with the pizza boxes. Before the door shut, he shouted, "Then starve."

Jun rushed back to the Crust Mobile, clutching the cash to her chest.

Get out of here.

Before her thoughts could get any worse, she shook her head, turned the key, and started down the road. The hours went by in a blur and by her last delivery she was completely drained. Alexa was still at the register when she returned the keys to the van.

"You okay?" Alexa asked.

Jun started and hid the motion by running a hand through her hair. "Yeah, I'm good now."

"What happened?" Alexa asked, raising a perfectly waxed eyebrow.

"Nothing. Just got this bad feeling about a customer." Jun sighed. "He didn't even do anything. Something just felt off." Really, he hadn't done anything wrong. Just sat near her in class and ordered pizza. Oh, and glared at her classmates and wrote about them in his murder book. But there wasn't anything criminal about that.

Alexa hesitated for a moment, considering her. "You know, I wouldn't take any chances. Trust your instincts. You don't want to realize that you were right and you should have listened to yourself. Here, take this. For if he bothers you again."

From her purse with the little gold chain, she took out a black tube with a bright yellow label. Mace.

Jun opened her mouth to protest. Mace was contraband, and she had her scholarship to think about. The words died when she saw the seriousness in Alexa's eyes.

"Hey, thanks," Jun said instead.

The bold warning labels had her second-guessing her decision as she placed it in a side pocket of her brand new teddy bear bag, but knowing it was there also put aside some of her worst fears. Most likely it would sit there for a week collecting lint before she'd return it.

"Don't mention it. And let me know if that asshole tries anything. I got your back, girl."

Jun smiled. Alexa wasn't half bad. "Right back at you. I'll see you tomorrow, then."

It was quiet as she walked toward the library. Mist surrounded the lampposts, and the air was cool in the fading light. Jun walked briskly, avoiding the trees and staying clear of the shadows stretching across the lawn. By now most of the night classes finished and there were only a few students left on campus. The same was true for the library.

As much as it had been an excuse, she told the truth to Bailey about working on the essay that night. Jun grabbed her normal spot in the back near the wall-length windows. This corner was secluded, with bookshelves to one side and a wall to the other. Jun sank into the plush armchair, the soft microfibers brushing against the back of her knees, before she pulled the table a smidgeon closer and got to work.

It was nearly impossible to focus in the dorm, what with Suzie sighing heavily and firing loaded glances her way. Either Jun was typing too loudly, or turning pages too indecisively, or taking too much of her side of the room, or whatever complaint of the day Suzie had.

She wouldn't be bothered here. She laid out her books carefully until her textbook, notebook, and her favorite pens were arranged just so. All right, perfect. While twirling her pen in her finger as she brainstormed the first three words of a killer intro sentence, she noticed Evan walk in. Though they attended the same courses for almost four years now, she'd never talked to him outside of class. She doubted he even knew her name.

He took a vacant table, and Jun turned her attention back to her essay. She was reworking the thesis, absently staring vaguely into space, lost in thought, when a shadow passed by the shelves. She thought nothing of it until he removed a few books just one shelf away from her and she saw him through the gap, separated by a thin row of books.

It was the stranger, Nikolai. Three times in one day? How could that even be a coincidence? He scanned outward across the library where the other students worked.

What was he doing here? If this were anyone else, she would say that he was just looking for one of his friends.

Remember, you have to trust your instincts.

Jun took a deep breath and looked back to her essay before Nikolai could notice her staring.

Before she could focus on writing, she heard the vibrations of a phone.

Jun reached for her pocket, cringing in horror. But her screen was blank.

"What? I'm busy," Nikolai muttered softly. Jun doubted she would have been able to hear him if she wasn't so close. "Campus library." He paused. "I have eyes on them now. This one hates Cartwright more than the others."

Nikolai's voice got even lower, more threatening. "I don't

know if he could have caused the quake. I'll let you know when I find out."

Did I hear that right? Caused the quake?

Was this some kind of terrorism? Some geological warfare or a bomb? She didn't know how it could have been. Jun had experienced an earthquake once before, and the campus earthquake felt like an earthquake.

There was no one in here that was anywhere near Cartwright at the time of the earthquake. The only one anywhere near him at the time was herself. But if that was what they were looking for, then that would lead them straight to...

The words swam together on the page as her heart pounded.

Just walk away. Now, before it's too late. Get up. Get up. Pretend you're in the wrong place.

Her pen dropped out of her shaking fingers, and the clatter as it fell to the desk was loud as an alarm.

How many words had she written? Four or five? That suddenly seemed like enough for the day. Jun gently closed her books and slipped them back into her bag, moving slowly, and absolutely not looking anywhere near Nikolai.

She snuck away as fast as she dared, knuckles clenched white on the straps of her bag.

Jun had nothing to do with the earthquake, but if Nikolai was searching, his path led straight to her.

5

The room smelled sharp of sweat and cleaning supplies. It made Nikolai's nose sting, and he wiped the perspiration beginning to drip down his face. The treadmill was set to a brisk jog.

Hunched over and elbows flopping, Evan worked out on the mat a few yards away.

Three days. Nikolai had spent three days following Evan and had gotten nothing but a headache. The guy had about as much magical ability as a wet noodle. Plus, he had terrible form. Shadowing Evan was a waste.

There had to be something he was missing.

His phone in the cup holder vibrated. Nikolai slowed down and took the headphones out from his ears. It was a text from Roman.

How's the lead going?

Nikolai stopped running completely. He used the sports towel hanging around his neck to dry his hands. Nikolai took one hard look at the back of Evan's head. He knew in his gut it wasn't him, but then what wasn't he seeing?

Roman didn't like to be kept waiting. His phone vibrated before Nikolai had the chance to reply.

See any more signs?

Nikolai typed back. *I have eyes on him now. Nothing yet.*

He was tempted to admit that this lead had gone nowhere. Of the names he'd written down in his notes, Evan was the most vocal about hating Cartwright. Which wasn't enough to prove he was the magician, and the other names that he'd followed were much the same. In essence, his strongest lead was a dead end. But Nikolai was so sure he'd been on to something when he'd picked the Business Analytics class.

All right. Give us his name and dorm. We'll test him.

Nikolai crossed the gym to the wall lined with weights and turned his workout music on. The burn of his muscles eased some of his frustration. While lifting dumbbells, Nikolai sent over Evan Campbell's personal information and typical schedule that he'd acquired these last few days.

He had enough. Nikolai headed back.

Students hung around campus, fooling around. One group was practicing their choreography routine. They were around his age, but their lifestyle was alien. One kid couldn't keep his pose and fell to the ground, laughing. So this was what people meant by the college experience. From what he'd seen, Nikolai wouldn't say he was missing out.

Of course, the major exception to this was college food. He was in fast food heaven. His teammates probably thought the same since they kept ordering out each night. It was odd that they hadn't tonight. He'd returned to find the apartment empty. By now, the others usually had ordered something. Nikolai frowned. Maybe they were eating out without inviting him; he wouldn't put it past them.

The fridge only had some leftovers and ketchup packets,

and Nikolai ate two slices of pizza cold. It was Pistachio's. No one else ordered artichokes, olives and banana peppers. The only other food to eat in the kitchen was the unopened bag of spoiling apples on top of the fridge. He took three with him to the sagging sofa in the living room and sat down, opening his bag and pulling the essays out.

He'd skimmed through the essays nearly a week ago when he'd first gotten them, but now he tried to read them with a critical eye. Immediately, he ran a hand through his hair. If he wanted to comb through paperwork, he would have taken a desk job. The content bored him to shit. Nothing stood out. He flipped back through the pile to Evan's, whose paper was a solid page shorter than the class average. Filled with typos, too—that was supposed to be 'assess' unless Evan really was talking about the clients' asses.

Nikolai thumbed through each paper. The familiar thought that he was missing something tugged at him. But this was useless. He didn't quite know what he was looking for. The professor hadn't even had time to mark any of the papers except one. On Bear's paper the professor wrote *15 minutes late*—that just seemed pointless to him.

Nikolai dropped the papers back into his bag when his phone vibrated. He looked at the screen.

428 Oakvale Ave.

A spike of excitement got his blood pumping. Finally, they were going to do something. Nikolai unlocked his suitcase, taking out his knives. He tilted one blade so that the light reflected off the sharpened edge. He felt at home as they slipped into hidden sheaths.

The address was in walking distance, and his GPS took him to a "For Sale" sign on a quiet residential street. It was a ranch style house with chipped paint. Renovation work didn't quite hide all the traces of fire damage to one side, in the blackened columns.

No point in walking up to the front window to check. He knew there wouldn't be anything to see. Nikolai walked around to the back, letting himself in through the unlocked fence. A window had been left open for him, and he pulled himself up and swung into the house.

He knew something was off from the smell. There was a hint of iron. It cut through the everyday scent of fresh paint and chemical cleaners in the dark, vacant rooms. Nikolai paused to release a knife, holding it at the ready.

He didn't have to ask them where they were. There was no sound quite like the sharp slap of fists pummeling flesh. He followed the noise, drifting in from a small room to the left. Roman and David were standing over a hog-tied figure while Pistachio leaned against the wall, texting.

Purple rings formed around swollen eyes, the bruising just visible under the blindfold. Nikolai could tell at a glance one or possibly both of his arms were dislocated. A puddle that was a mix of blood and mucus, tears and teeth sank into the beige carpet around his face.

Tied and beaten—it didn't matter. Nikolai recognized Evan immediately.

"Took you long enough." David straightened up and rolled the sleeves of his jacket newly adorned with splotches of bright red. He then looked down at his shoes and swore. "Got blood all over my new boots. You take a turn."

"No more," Evan sobbed directly into the carpet. Spittle bubbled with each slurred word. "Please... no more. I don't know what you want."

Nikolai didn't move. His grip on the handle was tight enough to feel the thudding of his pulse.

"Come on. He's not going to break himself," Roman said.

"Looks plenty broken to me." Pistachio didn't take his eyes off his cellphone screen.

Seeing Evan like this and knowing it was his own fault, Nikolai felt the guilt stab him, swift and gutting.

"It's not him," Nikolai said, his voice detached. "It's not Evan."

"What are you talking about, of course it's him. Maybe his face looks a little messed up, but it's the Evan kid," Roman corrected him.

"You know what I meant," Nikolai snapped.

Roman shrugged. He squatted down and pulled Evan's hair so his face wasn't pressed into the carpet. "So you said you had nothing to do with it?" He tightened his grip on Evan's hair. "That can't be true. You had to have done something to make my friend here suspicious of you."

Evan looked barely conscious, but the groan sounded like a no.

Nikolai's lip curled at the challenge in Roman's tone. "He was too interested in Cartwright's death, it didn't seem normal. So I followed him long enough to realize he was harmless. I had the situation under control. You didn't need to step in like this."

"But you still alerted us. Agreed that he needed testing." Roman narrowed his eyes.

Nikolai held Roman's gaze, refusing to admit that if he'd known this would happen, he would have kept his mouth shut. "I thought that the rest of the team might be able to find something I missed. You could have waited for me." Why did this feel like somehow it stopped being about Evan?

With a grunt of disgust, Roman released Evan's hair. He looked over to Pistachio. "You got this?"

Pistachio nodded. "I'll take care of it."

Roman took his leave, pausing to clasp Nikolai on his shoulder on the way out. "Next time, do a better job picking your target."

"It's no big deal, man." David gestured down to Evan on the floor as he followed Roman out. "We were all getting bored out of our minds anyway."

Nikolai waited until he heard the window ledge slide and the thud as they left the house before he turned to Pistachio and asked, "What's going to happen to him?"

"Don't worry about it." Pistachio was still glued to his phone.

"No." Nikolai dropped the stoic act. "This is my fault. I want to know what's going to happen to him."

Pistachio peeled his eyes away from his phone and gave him a hard look. "Got a guy coming. He should be here in another ten minutes or so. Ex-army medic. He'll be able to get him stable. Then we'll drug him and send him to some rehab facility in Reno. We'll be long gone before he gets out."

Nikolai ran his hand through his hair. Finally, Evan's loud shuddering breaths were giving way to unconsciousness. "Are they always like this?"

"It depends." Pistachio looked down at Evan, considering. "Today was actually rather mild. I'd say Evan is lucky to still be breathing."

By the way he said it, Nikolai could hear in his tone that there were probably quite a few unlucky people. Nikolai had to be sure. "If I hadn't said anything, would Evan be beaten to death?"

"Probably."

Nikolai let that sink in. They would have killed an innocent man.

This shouldn't have been a surprise to him. Of course,

if it meant catching the magician, some sacrifices were necessary. His father's words echoed back to him. *"Let me ask you a question. If you could go back in time and kill Hitler as a baby, would you do it? Most people would say that he should be killed as a baby, but let's be honest. How many of them could do it? You have to be stronger than everyone else. You have to make the hard choices, because no one else is going to."*

Killing one magician meant saving thousands of lives. It had to be done. But he never quite imagined taking a civilian's life. "You knew he wasn't the magician?"

"Not at first, but it became obvious quite quickly," Pistachio said.

"Then why didn't you stop them?"

"It's not so simple." Pistachio sighed. He flattened back the curly hair he had in a topknot. "Roman should be the one telling you this." He shook his head, a wry smile forming. "But we can't afford to be too careful. We've got to keep moving and catch this guy before the next earthquake. Before the entire campus goes down."

Nikolai held his tongue. As he was new to the team, he couldn't go off on them and start saying their logic was fucked—it was possible to find the magician without casualties, if they were smart about it. He wouldn't say anything; he would just have to do it.

"If you don't feel you're up for this, tell Roman you want out."

"No, I understand." And he did. He'd always known there were ugly aspects to this work. Hands would inevitably get dirty, but that didn't mean he had to do things their way.

"Good. Now, if you'll excuse me, I have a high score I need to beat." Pistachio unlocked his phone.

Evan was unconscious, his body too still for comfort, when Nikolai stepped out.

He needed to think. He let the cool air clear his head as he started walking.

In the muted light of dusk, the campus was quiet. These dorm buildings and classrooms were filled with innocent people—and the magician who could kill them all.

Catching the magician couldn't wait. Yet, Evan was innocent. Why wasn't that obvious to the others? He didn't return to their shared apartment till the first rays of dawn.

There was little to discover in the next few days. He read the pile of essays enough times that the business facts started to actually make sense, and yet he learned nothing else from them. His old notes pointed to dead ends. By now, the construction work on Cartwright's office had cleared away any remaining evidence. He'd examined the newly built floor, searched through the old man's desk, and found nothing of interest. Only papers, books, and framed photos of dogs. Whatever trail there might have been was wiped clean, which left him with very little.

But he wasn't ready to give up on the Business Analytics class. He got there early when Tuesday rolled by and sat way in the back. It was more important than ever to pay attention to every detail. But Nikolai didn't have to go looking for new events unfolding, not when they were parading right in front of his face. One guy Nikolai had initially dismissed as non-threatening walked toward him. Nikolai sized him up as he approached. Decent musculature, simple yet expensive clothing. Bailey, his memory supplied. Bailey Allen.

It was about time someone came to ask what he was doing here. Nikolai ran through different phrases he could use to keep his cover. Bailey didn't strike him as a magician, but a confrontation could attract the wrong sort of attention.

To keep his eye on the class, he had to appear legitimate. Now he'd see how good Pistachio's forgery was, and how good his transfer student excuse would hold.

Bailey walked into his row and Nikolai reflexively tensed, only to relax again when he walked past him a few seats down, standing in front of the purple hat girl. "Hey, did you finish that essay?"

"Not yet, I couldn't get into it," she said.

"Why don't you come over to my place? We could work on it together."

"Umm." From the corner of his eye, he could see her fidget in her seat. "Yeah. I could do that. That works."

"Do you still have my number?"

"It's somewhere." She blushed and bent down into her bag.

"Here." He held his palm out, and she handed him a pink phone with fluffy keychains. He typed out a quick message and clicked send. "Text me when you're free."

If he wasn't so close, it would just seem like this Bailey guy only wanted to work on his essay. But Nikolai noted his dilated pupils, the lingering smile. He was interested in her, and just got her number. *Smooth.*

And definitely not what he was supposed to be looking for. Nikola's eye twitched. Just more normal college stuff.

Bailey returned to his seat, passing by him on his way. If money had a smell, it would be whatever expensive cologne he was wearing.

The class was beginning to turn into another disappointment. They had a boring lesson and then a short quiz at the end, and Nikolai didn't even bother reading after the first question. *How does the collection of Big Data allow businesses to infer human intent in data analysis?* It was a measure of how much time he spent in the class that he actually understood the question, and if pressed would have been able to write out a partial answer. He jotted the occasional word down so that it wasn't obvious that he wasn't actually answering the questions, and instead continued to pay attention to the class, even though it was clear there wasn't going to be anything to see.

In the third row, there was a guy frantically erasing an answer and scraping away the rubbings, then gnawing his pencil like a dog. Another student was literally breathing hard as he tapped a pencil against his leg. There were students with visible signs of anxiety and tension over something as ridiculous as showing off whether they knew the answer to some random questions. They had to join this century. None of this mattered. People could just google anything they needed to know.

Nikolai looked out of the corners of his eyes for any signs of a magician. Perhaps this quiz was nerve-wracking enough to flush the magician out. Nikolai almost rolled his eyes at that. He dutifully scanned the room and was not surprised when he once again found nothing out of the normal.

The first handful of students turned in their quizzes, grabbed their things, and walked out the door. Nikolai was considering doing the same when he noticed that one of the students who finished hung back by the door. It took him a moment to place the tall guy who seemed stretched thin. Louis, he thought it was. Louis watched another student, still in his seat, who checked over his answers for the third time.

It wasn't until the other student turned in his test that Louis finally spoke. Though he tried to speak in a low voice, the acoustics of the room, designed like an amphitheater, managed to carry his words all the way across to the back of the room clearly. "Hey, have you seen Evan? He's not answering his phone or anything. I was hoping that he would at least make it to class."

"Maybe he's just taking a break or something."

"His roommate says that he hasn't been back in four days, and his girlfriend's freaking out. Evan wouldn't just leave like that. Something must have happened."

Then Nikolai felt it: the air pulling tight, like the bowstring of an arrow drawn back, about to be let loose. Nikolai clenched the wooden arms of his chair. This was magic capable of much worse than a 6.5 earthquake and one injury. He braced himself in the case of a quake, scanning down the rows in front of him for any sign of a magician at work.

There were too many people, and all of them could be crushed to death if the building collapsed. This was exactly what he wanted to avoid. If he stopped the magician before the magic spiraled out of control, he could limit the amount of casualties.

Then the lights went out. Everyone was plunged into a deep darkness. There was a pause for a beat before a worried murmur took over the class. Cell phone lights flashed around the room. Nikolai knew this was the moment he could strike; his aim with the knife would be deadly. If only he had a target.

Almost as soon as the pressure in the air started, it faded away. Nikolai felt the charged air around the room recoil and disappear, vanishing like mist. The lights flickered back on. Immediately he tried to identify the source, but it was impossible with everyone looking around, talking in hushed voices while their spineless professor tried to calm the students. The class began to settle once more, though a lot of students quickly packed their belongings to leave. Maybe they could feel it, the unsettling shift in the air. Or smell the burnt ozone.

It was strange, though. He never experienced anything quite like this. When magic was built up to that strength and caliber, it typically rampaged into mass destruction. This was something else. This magician was nothing like the others he'd taken down in the past.

The magician was still in the room, that was clear, but there was nothing Nikolai could do without causing a scene and putting everyone here at risk. Not only that, but it would be foolish to make a move without backup. It would be safer to alert the others, let them know what he had seen. Even if it was too obvious to have all of them hanging out in one classroom, it would help to have them out in the halls, or another set of eyes to be on alert.

As he picked up his cell phone to alert Roman, he thought of Evan's bloody face being lifted from the carpet. No. This time there would be no mistake about who the magician was.

Nikolai kept a watchful eye on the students who got up and turned in their papers to the front. He crossed out the names he was sure left early and tried to retrace the events that transpired. The pulse was triggered right after the other boys were talking about Evan—so the magician must have known something about Evan. Maybe a friend who only just found out about his disappearance.

A sudden, daunting thought occurred to him. It was quite possible whoever it was knew they were being hunted and that meant they knew who he was.

Nikolai remained for a minute, feeling like a sitting duck, as things went back to normal, as if nothing happened at all. As more and more of them turned in the quiz, Nikolai had no way of knowing whether or not the magician was still there, or if they had already left. When only a few students remained, and someone was asking the professor a question, he silently left out the back.

Outside, it was already dark. The sky was struck through with heavy clouds, which cast a gloom about everything. Yet, even here a small crowd gathered, looking up at the sky. Some students were pointing, and others had their cell-phones recording.

"What the hell was that?"

"It's over there."

Nikolai followed their pointed gazes in time to see a flash of light bloom across the sky in a massive blue orb. All around him, students were chattering excitedly, asking if others got it on film, stating that they were going to post it on Snapchat.

Earthquake lights. He had only seen them in pictures before. Scientists couldn't explain them, had no explanation for the phenomenon, but he knew what they were. These lights were formed out of the residue of magic. Nikolai looked around at all the smartphones out documenting the lights and shook his head. Soon everyone who knew the truth about magic would be alerted with this huge signal across the sky.

If Nikolai wanted to find this magician on his own, he would need to work fast. Things were getting more complicated.

6

"Hey, Pickles," Jun crooned, opening up the wire cage that took up an entire quarter of the room. Pickle Berry hopped straight into the palm of her hand, and Jun lifted him up to her shoulder. She reached for a packet of assorted treats and picked a nice fat sunflower seed. Pickles grasped it in both tiny hands and started munching.

Since last weekend, Jun had crocheted an assortment of mini accessories. She just hadn't had the time for an update. Jun balanced a tiny wool top hat on his head and snapped a quick picture before it toppled off. "That's perfect, Pickles, you're going to be a star." The props changed, and Pickles now balanced a pointed wizard cap between his ears. Jun placed a miniature wand in front of him. "Come on, Pickles, you can do it." Pickles grabbed the wand in his tiny fingers. Picture perfect.

It was hard to be discerning, as her faithful pet always looked so darn adorable, but she managed to select the best pics for Instagram. She skimmed through her app to find that she had gained twenty-three followers since she last checked. She tried not to let the fame get to her head—even though she owned the third most popular chinchilla on the internet.

Jun poured some chinchilla dust into the pickle jar—an actual cleaned out Costco jar that had once housed pickles. Her little buddy hopped in and started rolling in his dust bath. His movements were as enthusiastic as they were twitchy. Little clouds of dust emerged from the jar like the ash bellowing out of an active volcano.

Noises came from the kitchen. Her father always made French toast for her weekend visits, and it was glorious—just the right combination of crisp and buttery, along with generous helpings of both syrup and cinnamon.

With Pickles back in his cage, she went to the kitchen to set the table.

"So, what's new?" Her father asked as they began to eat.

Jun swallowed. There was so much she couldn't mention. *Hey, Dad, a kid just disappeared from my cohort. And the creepy imposter who probably murdered him sits next to me in class. Nothing to worry about.* What was a nice, calm topic she could use to distract him from all that? Jun twirled her spoon around the mini lake of syrup pooling at the bottom of her plate when the thought struck. Bailey.

"Well, there's this guy." Jun kept her eyes fixed on her toast, suddenly embarrassed at the drawn-out way she started. "He gave me his number and asked if we could work on the paper together."

Her father put down his fork. "Yeah? And what did you say?"

"I said it was all right. I was getting around to texting him."

"Well, go on, text him now, then. He's probably been waiting for you."

Jun sighed. Had she just dug herself into a hole? "It's not like *that*. It's just for class."

"Oh, Jun Berry, a boy isn't going to give you his number just to work on some essay."

Jun's cheeks flushed, the warmth making her stomach itch. She thought that might be the case but had convinced herself into believing otherwise. "Then I should probably make some sort of excuse."

"Oh, what's the matter? Does he have a big nose and ears that stick out?"

She couldn't help the small grin as he used his hands to cup around his ears. "He's not an elephant, Dad." *Far from it.* "I barely know the guy." At his look, Jun continued, "Plus, I'll be graduating in a few months. I don't want to be distracted."

There was a pause. Her father went quiet and ate his French toast in silence. Jun wondered if that was the end of it.

"You know, when I first met your mother in college, I didn't think I'd have a chance," her father admitted softly. Jun's eyes widened in shock. He usually avoided talking about her. "But she said yes." He laughed, his eyes bright from the memory. "So, who knows, maybe things will work out with this guy."

Jun bit her lip at the sight of that smile. If it wasn't for her, he would have been able to smile more often. Her father rarely asked her for anything. Jun caused him to worry too often.

"Fine. It wouldn't hurt just to text him," she said. The worst that could happen would be getting caught up on her assignment. She scrolled through her contacts and fired off a quick text.

Hey, you still want to write that paper?

Jun was about to put her phone back down, but frowned at the sight of the three dots at the bottom of her screen showing he was typing back.

Perfect timing. I just got back from the gym. I'm free now.

Jun frowned at her cellphone. Now? "He says he's free, but I can't hang out with him now."

"What are you talking about? Of course you can." He had a playful gleam in his eyes, the dad look.

"I was going to hang out with you."

"Well, I'm going fishing. The trout are really biting." He got up from the table and made a beeline to his tackle-box in the drawer. He jammed his bucket hat on his head. "Gotta go."

"Dad!"

He grabbed his car keys off the kitchen counter and gave Jun a wave. "Tell me all about it."

He shut the door, leaving Jun alone with a breakfast plate smeared in syrup.

Jun groaned, leaned back in her chair, and stared up at the ceiling. This was not how she pictured her day. After a minute of weighing her options, she sighed and grabbed her phone.

I can be there in 30.

Jun parked a good two blocks away from the apartment complex and pulled up the emergency brake on Old Faithful, the Nissan Sentra that was older than she was.

She took a deep breath. "It's just an essay," she reminded herself. "No big deal." She repeated the sentiment as she passed the koi pond in the front lobby, and again as she walked down the marble hallway.

Her finger hovered by the intricate wood panels of Bailey's door. Well, it was either face Bailey, or her father's disappointed questions later. Jun rang the doorbell.

Bailey answered the door in a well fitted t-shirt and shorts. Jun forced herself to look at his face. She told herself it was because she was so used to seeing him in more professional clothes. It didn't mean anything.

"Hey, come on in. Make yourself at home." He smiled. It was a rather nice smile, and not just because of the full lips or the straight white teeth. The warmth behind Bailey's smile appealed to Jun.

"Thanks," Jun replied. She stepped into the room, and at the sight of the books and papers already laid out across the leather ottoman, she gave herself a mental shake. This had to be from all of her father's talk. She had to remember that she had actual work to do.

The room was well furnished, cleaner than she expected. Everything complimented, from the cream-colored upholstery to the gray throw rug in front of the leather sofa. It had a minimal but expensive touch. "It's a nice place you got," she said as she took out her own books and computer.

"Thanks, it's all right. Can I get you anything? I've got water, tea, coffee?"

"Coffee, please."

"Good choice. I just got a new drip coffee maker. It's really the only thing keeping me alive at this point."

When he brought her the piping hot cup, Jun sighed into it. It was divine, sharp and bright, with undertones of caramel. The time went by smoothly in addition to the occasional refills of excellent coffee. While swapping ideas, Jun managed to write the rough draft of her essay. It helped to get a second opinion.

She was reading through another article when Bailey asked, "What are you going to do after graduation?"

"I want to open up my own business."

Bailey smiled one of those warm, genuinely interested smiles. "Oh, we got an entrepreneur in here. What kind of business?"

Jun brushed a stray strand of hair behind her ear. It was always a little embarrassing to admit. "Um. A craft store."

But Bailey only nodded. "Ah, of course. The hat." He pointed to her purple hat she knitted last break. "It looks great."

"Thanks. And you? What are your plans?"

Bailey took a deep, considering breath. "Nothing interesting. I'm doing this because it's expected of me. Carry on the family business and all. My dad owns a couple restaurants and properties. He's waiting for me to take over so he can retire early. The old man just wants to sit on a beach with a Piña Colada."

"So he's counting down the days till your graduation?"

"Exactly, more so than me." Bailey laughed, then checked the clock. "Wow, has it really been three hours? No wonder I'm starving. You know, there's this new Chinese place I've been dying to try. I could really use some brain food."

Chinese? Jun hadn't had any in weeks. "Yeah, Chinese sounds good. I've been getting sick of pizza." One more slice of stale pizza might even be enough to drive her mad.

"Blasphemy."

"You try eating pizza every day, then come talk to me."

"All right, maybe I will. After I order us some take out."

The food came fifteen minutes later, delivered to his door. There were three plastic bags, including a container of Egg Drop soup. Bailey practically bought the whole menu.

"Were you planning on feeding a small army, too?"

"I wasn't sure what you'd like." Bailey carefully opened containers of spring rolls, beef with broccoli, sweet and sour pork, salt and pepper prawn, Kung Pao chicken, fried rice and chow mein. It smelled heavenly.

They talked about their professors and their classes as they ate. Nothing went wrong. No cooking meant nothing caught on fire. The cat didn't try to use her as a scratching post. Just good food and good conversation. Bailey was so easy to talk with.

It was actually almost like a date.

Settled into the beginnings of her food coma, Jun cracked open her fortune cookie without thinking of it. She didn't look up when Bailey laughed and read aloud his fortune. "The stars shine bright on you tonight. You will find love, and he will be handsome and rich... I think I picked the wrong fortune. What does yours say?"

The paper in her hand had a single word.

Run.

Bailey leaned over and read it. "Run, huh? Never seen that before."

She crumpled the paper and tossed it on the table. "I probably need to after eating all those carbs."

But Jun couldn't help frowning at the tiny ball of crumpled paper. An unsettling feeling prickled in the back of her throat, leaving her feeling jittery, but Jun swallowed it down. It was just a stupid fortune like all the others. It didn't mean anything.

"If you need someone to run with," Bailey said with a grin, "I could keep you company."

Jun smiled back, grateful for the distraction. "Are you recruiting me into your fitness routine?"

"Something like that."

"In that case, I might need some more carbs," June said, and she ate the pieces of her fortune cookie. She checked the time on her phone and sighed. "I actually do have to run. I got work." She normally didn't work weekends, but Antonio practically begged her after one of the other girls called out sick.

"Thanks for inviting me over," Jun said as she gathered her things.

"We should do it again sometime. You know, if you're up to it."

She couldn't deny his hopeful grin. Neither did she have to lie or find an excuse to say otherwise. "Yeah, I'd like that."

Her good mood stayed with her until she began to deliver pizza, and then it evaporated completely. The higher tips working on a Saturday did not make up for the college aged boys who thought waving money at her entitled them to something.

"No, my number is not included with your order," Jun said with a tense smile frozen on her face—a testament to her years of experience in customer service.

Many of her customers recognized that smile as professional courtesy.

Mr. Shattuck Ave. did not.

"Want the best sex of your life?" he asked while she handed him his box. He purposely reached further to feel her hand.

"No." She stepped away, wiping the back of her hands on her pants.

"Then I'm the guy for you." He winked.

Now's the time to run.

She did, all the way to the Crust Mobile. Behind the wheel, Jun shook her head. This was ridiculous. She was listening to a cookie. What was wrong with her? She headed back to Feelin' Saucy to collect the next batch of pizzas.

Jun went through two more drop offs, but because of roadwork and traffic, the last four boxes of this delivery were cooling down fast. She parked in front of an old laundromat and hastily rounded the corner. It wasn't until she'd rang the doorbell and was waiting in front of the heavy wooden door with the green chipping paint that she realized the laundromat seemed familiar.

1306. Nikolai lived here.

The floorboards creaked as someone heavy descended the stairs.

Jun backed up a few steps. Should she just drop the pizzas and run back to the van? Except—it was too late. The door already jostled as someone undid the locks. Jun froze as the door opened and she kept her head down, hair and cap slanted over her eyes. She lifted the box with the flimsy hope that he would be too interested in the pizza to notice her.

His gaze swept over her indifferently as he eyed the boxes of pizzas in her hand. "So that's four large pizzas. Pepperoni, the margarita, the sausage with extra cheese, and the ridiculous order with the anchovies, onion, and broccoli?"

He looked at her expectantly, and Jun realized that he was waiting for her.

"Yes, it's all there. Fifty-nine, eighty-one, please."

He took the boxes and dug into his sweatpants for the folded-up bills. When he held out the money, palm up with healed over calluses, Jun reached for it. Her thumb brushed coarse, leather-thick skin as she wrapped her hands around the bills, and she felt the shock—static that shot up through her arm. She jerked her hand away, the money held tight in her fist. For a moment she dared to hope she'd been the only one to feel it.

Nikolai stared at her, first wide-eyed, then narrowed.

This close, it was impossible to ignore the rigid set of his jaw or the thick muscles tightening.

Something in the pit of her stomach dropped, and the same jittery feeling itched under her skin and raised the fine hairs at the back of her neck.

Shit.

Jun took a step back, as if that small measure of space was going to do anything.

Nikolai frowned, his eyes sweeping across her features. "All right, thanks," he finally said, closing the door on her.

Breathing hard like she ran miles rather than the few yards from Nikolai's house to her escape vehicle, Jun was soon on the road and down the street.

She stopped short at a red light, jamming her foot on the break. The Crust jerked to a halt, and the cars behind her honked. Jun checked the rear-view windows, sure the face of the driver in every car would be his. When she released her tight grip on the steering wheel to turn the radio on, her unsteady fingers flipped the window wipers.

When he recognized her, she thought he'd have done something, maybe grab her and pull her up the stairs. Had she been wrong about him and Evan's disappearance? The way her stomach twisted told her otherwise.

Somehow, on autopilot, she found her way back to Feelin' Saucy. She turned off the engine and sighed. Her arms were numb from gripping the steering wheel. Little crescent shapes were embedded in her palms. All around her were students, nothing out of the ordinary. Her shift was over, and in another forty-five minutes, she'd be eating sushi with her dad.

Alexa nodded at her as Jun returned the keys. Was Alexa wrong about the whole instinct thing? Had this all been in her head?

The streetlamps glowed orange, mimicking the hazy sunset lingering behind the buildings. While walking, she texted her dad that her shift was over. He saw the message and already began typing a response. Probably asking for all the details about her 'date.'

Jun unlocked her car and just as she was opening the door, a hand shot out from behind, grabbing her wrist with enough force to bruise. Before she could even think to do something—wrench her arm free, blow the horn, scream— she was shoved to the passenger seat, her face pressed into the door panel, hands forced behind her back as if she weighed nothing. Jun craned her head back for a glimpse. She'd been wrong. Nikolai had been waiting for her.

A sharp blow struck the back of her head, and her thoughts faded into the darkness.

7

The junk car rattled as Nikolai pressed the accelerator, its engine groaning so the whole street could hear. Though his eyes were on the road, his focus was on the girl seated next to him. His knife, sheathed at his belt, was ready for the first hint of magic.

Nikolai knew that choosing to act alone was incredibly stupid. Hell, it could get him—or worse, a whole lot of innocent people—killed. Except he couldn't alert the others just yet. Not when he wasn't completely sure himself.

Unconscious, she looked so damn vulnerable. Barely ninety pounds, soft features. She even owned a bag shaped like a teddy bear. Nothing like any magician he'd seen before. If he hadn't felt that sharp zap of magic himself, he'd swear it was the wrong girl. Nikolai shook his head. But she was in Cartwright's class. One of the two girls in attendance. The one who knit.

That couldn't be a coincidence.

The car strained up the steep incline of the California hills, the engine's racket getting louder as the light of the sun disappeared below the horizon. He hadn't made it to their destination when her eyes started to flutter. Wincing, she came to. With her arms tied behind her back, it took some twisting for her to get up.

Nikolai rested his finger on his blade, bracing for her reaction. Earthquake on the road. Toss the car off course—a crash could kill him as fast as magic.

The girl looked to the dashboard on the car, leaning closer and blinking at the numbers.

"Shit," she muttered.

Fumbling with her tied hands, she patted her side pocket.

"Shit," she repeated.

She faced him, and Nikolai let his index finger slide out the handle of the blade.

"I need to call my father," she said. It was urgent enough to be a demand.

Nikolai tensed his hand on the wheel. Whatever she was trying to pull, he wasn't falling for it.

"Nikolai, please."

"How do you know my name?" There was no record of it in the system. The only way she'd know would be from some means of magic. It was sloppy work for her to know his name when he couldn't recall hers.

"I delivered you pizza," she said flatly. "Maybe next time don't have it shouted from the second floor. Look, my dad's going to be worried. I was supposed to meet him two hours ago for sushi."

Sushi? Was this girl for real? "That's not going to happen."

She was quiet long enough for Nikolai to wonder if maybe she was still dazed from the blow before she spoke again. "He's seventy-three and has had two heart attacks already. I'm not going to do anything. I just can't let him worry."

Her words trailed away, and moisture gathered in the corner of her eyes.

Nikolai pulled out his phone, knowing it was stupid. There was no way this girl was some normal civilian. She was taking this far too well. She had to be planning something. Even if she hadn't immediately blasted him apart, she must still be planning to kill him. With one hand on the wheel and the other holding out the phone, it would take an extra six seconds to access his blade. God, he was an idiot. "What's his number?"

She blinked at him, before reeling off the numbers slowly while he punched them in.

It rang on speaker twice before someone picked up. "Hello?" asked a shaky voice.

"Hey, Dad." She sounded different. Relieved.

"Jun Berry! What happened? Is everything all right?"

Jun Berry? Jun Bear.

Ranked seventh in the class. No conduct records. Nikolai had written her off.

"Yeah, it's nothing. My phone died at the library and I had to borrow one. It's that essay I wrote. I read the prompt wrong. I was trying to fix it real quick. I mean. I could just pull an all-nighter and still make it over to you."

"No, no, no. Little Berry, I don't want you to have to do that. Take care of that essay."

"But I would rather see you."

"I know how important this degree is to you. We can get dinner to celebrate your graduation."

"Okay, love you, Dad." Her voice hitched and she bit her lip, looking away.

"Love you."

The call ended, and Jun sighed. She turned back around, looking out the window.

What was she doing? Most likely it was a ploy to distract him, but why would she need to? He pressed on the gas harder, and the car lurched forward.

Nikolai gritted his teeth as the engine began to churn and smoke escaped from the hood. He had no choice but to pull over to the side of the road and turn the car off.

He got out and went around to her side. She shrank back when he opened the door. "Did you do this?" he demanded.

You're kidding me? Her expression was as obvious as if she said the words out loud. "No. You did this," Jun said. "You completely shot the accelerator."

The car was still smoking, and he couldn't waste time getting it to run. Beyond the guardrails were the woods. Isolated enough. It would have to do.

"Nice going, by the way. Did they teach you how to drive in kidnap school?" Jun muttered under her breath.

She was still pretending to be normal. Fine. He could play along with her little game.

Nikolai pulled her out of the car. "Walk."

After the first few rows of trees, visibility dimmed, and then they were stepping in blind. Nikolai kept her ahead of him, pushing her forward every time she paused. Any second she could slither out of the rope tying her wrists. He waited for her to make a run for it.

They were far enough for the road to disappear from view. The lingering heat from being in the car faded fast, and the nighttime air was chilling. From the smell of rot and bog, they must have been nearing a swamp or lake. Thick dirt began to soften, and his shoes sunk in mud in areas. In the distance, water reflected back at him.

Through the thinning tree branches, the moon broke free of the clouds. Nikolai held his hand against her back, keeping her moving. He felt her shiver.

The trees dispersed, cut off suddenly by a ravine. Fifteen feet or so below them was a lake. Now, in the dark, it gave the impression of a cliffside. He didn't want to drag this any further, and this was the perfect spot for what he had in mind.

"You still won't admit it, then." Nikolai watched her intently. He fully expected her to flee or fight now that she was cornered. He stepped closer to her, and Jun backed up until she was right at the edge.

"Admit what?" she snapped, with a slight tremor that rattled her teeth.

"What you are." Nikolai waited for a look of guilt, understanding, anything. When it was clear that she wasn't going to say a word, he pushed her, hard enough that she stumbled back over the ledge.

She screamed as she fell. A scream ending abruptly with a splash. And then silence. Nikolai waited, watching the black water churn for a few rapid heartbeats. It would be child's play for a magician to break out of those bonds and escape. He braced himself for her retaliation—it would come any minute now. There was no flash of lightning. No earthquake. No odd haze obscuring his vision.

There was nothing on the surface of the water but the ever-widening ring of ripples, spreading out from the spot where the water swallowed Jun up.

The water stilled completely. Seconds passed. Nikolai was tense, waiting. Wondering if this was just a trick. Until that uncertainty gave way to a weightier thought—how long had she been under the water? Longer than a magician would take to break free, but also longer than it would take any average swimmer to make it to the surface.

"Damn it."

It had been too long. Too long even for a trap.

Nikolai dove in after her.

8

Jun's stomach lurched as she was pushed, the impact sent her reeling backward. For a full second, she had a clear view of the night sky, stars swimming in her vision. And then she broke the surface.

Cold pierced her, first enveloping her with pain before leaching away at her strength. Panicked, Jun gulped for air and inhaled water. Immediately she tried to cough it out, but there was nothing but more water to replace it with. Agony seized her lungs and clawed her throat. She tried to kick, jerk her tied arms free, see through the black water surrounding her, but all she managed to do was arch in awkward circles. The water was everywhere. It slowed her thrashing limbs.

She was going to die. She knew it then. Dread seemed to seep to her bones, sinking her further. With her remaining strength, she kicked wildly, but in reality, it was mere twitches. It didn't matter anyway since it was impossible to tell where the surface was, her awareness already fading.

It wasn't cold anymore. Her burning lungs quieted down. As her struggles stopped, Jun drifted, and the water was gentle, taking her deeper. The darkness pressed in from all around until it was the only thing left.

Then it was forced out of her. A harsh pressure blew past her throat into her lungs, reigniting all her raw pain. Chasing away the fog in her mind. It all came out, brackish water and stomach acid, down her front. Jun had just enough mind to twist to the side, though the movement felt oddly sluggish. She breathed in thin streams of air, wrestling and pulling each ragged bit into her body. Each cough wracked her body. Her waterlogged lungs hurt as if they were being squeezed. Jun fell flat on her back, realizing after a moment she was no longer in the water. She concentrated on the soothing feel of air against the sting of acid at her throat.

Then she heard the crunch of leaves by her head, and Jun finally recognized the black shape above her as Nikolai. There was no further energy for her to move, let alone run like her mind was screaming at her to do. Her whole body shook from the exhaustion and the cold. He may have pulled her out of the water, but it wasn't to save her. No. She knew he had much worse things in store for her.

Another branch snapped, this time a few feet away. It took her a few moments searching in the dark to realize he was no longer there. It was her chance to escape, maybe her only one. She forced herself to move, and her leg dragged against the dirt like a log. She twisted to her side, but that alone caused her muscles to give out. Still she tried, even as she scraped against the forest floor, gasping.

If she disappeared, then her dad would worry himself into an early grave. She couldn't do that to him, not after what she'd done to her mother. The guilt pushed her forward, inching blindly along jagged rocks. She tried to dig her nails into the flesh of the earth, pulling herself forward with a raw desperation, but she couldn't force her numb fingers to grip properly.

A breeze drifted through the trees, chilling her damp clothes, as if she wore ice. Too soon, she heard the crunch of returning steps. Jun stifled a groan of bitter disappointment as she rested her forehead against the dirt and let herself slip off into exhaustion.

The crackle of fire jostled her awake. She gasped, adrenaline pounding through her as she drew away, certain she was about to be eaten by the flames. It took a moment for her panicked mind to register that she wasn't burning. She was dry. Warm.

She propped up onto her elbows and looked wildly around, her eyes slowly adjusting to the dark. The fire was just about down to embers. Pink streaks lined the horizon. How long had she been out here? She reached for her cellphone before recalling with sudden clarity the precise moment when it tumbled out of her hand. Even during a kidnapping, she registered seeing her newly paid off smartphone tumble, hitting the ground with a sharp crack.

"Took you long enough," Nikolai muttered. He was sitting across from her, just the low flames of a long-burning campfire between them.

Her entire body recoiled. She jerked herself upright, her feet scrabbling, kicking paths through the soil, before wobbling unsteadily to her feet. The world seemed to be spinning, and Jun reached for a tree, nearly stumbling into the peeling bark as her balance slanted.

The light from the fire didn't quite reach his face, casting him in shadow. "Don't bother, I'll just chase you down."

She tried anyway. One step back, and then a few more when she found her legs could support her weight.

"You really think you can outrun me?"

A guy his size? Not likely, but there was a chance she could lose him in the dark. She turned. The trees around her were barely visible. She wasn't a few feet away before her arm was grabbed.

"Get off me!" She yanked back to no avail, his grip as unrelenting as a bear trap. "Please, just let me go." She was forcibly returned to the fire's edge.

"Are we going to sit down and talk, or are we going to do this the hard way?"

"What's the hard way?" She continued to tug against his hold until his next words.

"The other method involves burying you."

Jun stilled.

At her nod, Nikolai dropped his hold. Jun glared into the fire as she sat, holding her knees. Burying her? What did that even mean? Was he just going to kill her? Or bury her alive? The guy didn't even have a shovel. "What do you want with me?"

Nikolai returned to the log across the fire where he had been before. "I'm still figuring that out. Depends on how you answer the next questions."

She nodded, slow and reluctant.

"Can you tell me about your midterm?"

What? Was this some kind of a joke? "I wrote a paper comparing different business models."

"What happened when you turned it in?"

Jun blinked a few times, finally meeting his eyes across the fire. "Regular class was cancelled. We just dropped off the papers."

"Then why was yours marked fifteen minutes late?"

How the hell did he know that? What exactly was he getting at? "I dropped it in a puddle on the way to class. I had to go home and reprint it."

Sparks and ash puffed out as he prodded the remaining fire. "What happened to students with late papers?"

"Cartwright had this policy, turn in the paper late and he would have taken off forty percent. I was going to lose my scholarship. I'd have to drop out or take on debt that I'd probably never be able to pay back."

This seemed to get his attention, his stare unwavering. "Were you angry at him?"

"No. I wasn't angry. I don't know, I was sort of panicked."

"And this was right before the earthquake, right?"

The way he said it was like he knew. There was no lying now. "I suppose it was."

"So you were there with him when it happened?"

She recalled Professor Cartwright, his paper-thin skin with tiny blue veins around his hard eyes that were looking down at her as the door closed. Seconds later was the earthquake. He couldn't have been a few feet away. When she saw him next, his body was unmoving, a corpse spread out on his desk. She closed her eyes from the image of it. "Well, not exactly. He was in his office."

"Can you tell me about a different time you were that panicked?"

Maybe it was because her dying professor was still in her thoughts or the entire pointless question, but it made her bristle. "I don't know? What does this have to do with anything?"

"Think."

It was easier to stare at the low flames than at him as she thought. When was the last time? She hadn't been that panicked in years. It was hard to remember, partially because a lot of those times were unpleasant memories buried in the hopes to be forgotten. She went through her high school years. Back amongst those linoleum floors and buzzing fluorescent lights. Surrounded by rows of scratched lockers and smudged whiteboards. The memory struck with all of the fury of teenage hormones. Four years later, it was still strong enough to make Jun's cheeks flush. "It's stupid."

Nikolai said nothing, his look expectant, and Jun sighed. "It wasn't actually anything serious. I just..." Jun trailed off. She took a deep breath, not wanting to be murdered for her silence. "I realized that I had blood" —her face felt even hotter— "on my pants."

"Whose was it?"

She shook her head. Forget about being murdered, now she was hoping the earth would open and swallow her whole so she wouldn't have to say any more. Despite the fact that it was just the two of them, Jun lowered her voice. "It was mine."

"You were panicked because you had hurt yourself?"

How could a guy be this willfully dense? "No, it was just a stupid mistake. I sort of lost track of time." She took one look at his blank face and realized he really was in fact going to make her say it. "Of the month."

"Oh." It took him a full second before it actually hit. "*Oh.*" He shifted on his log and looked away from her for the first time since the start of the conversation.

Jun looked away as well and wondered if it would feel better if she was simply struck dead now.

"What happened after?" He made a fruitless gesture. "You know."

"No one noticed because right after the power went out in the school and we had the rest of the day off."

"Really, now? Did the power go off frequently?"

Jun frowned in thought. "I guess. At least once a year."

"Then can you tell me about another time the power went out?"

There was the time it went off right as a guy ran into the girls' locker room as they were changing for gym. The ensuing chaos and shrieking in the dark brought their gym teacher in, who everyone suspected was a perv, but she wasn't going to embarrass herself any further. It took another few moments for her to dig further. "Students a few grades above me were fighting in the halls. They were getting violent and a few others got hurt trying to stop them. Not even the teacher could stop them. Luckily the power went off when it did."

"Uh-huh. And did anything worse than the power going out happen while you were at school?"

There had been worse. "Yeah, maybe some old ceiling tiles broke, but it was an old building. Things needed to be replaced decades ago."

"All of those accidents and not once did you think that maybe it wasn't a coincidence?"

Jun hesitated, caught off guard. "What do you mean?"

"That every time you were panicked, something happened," Nikolai said with complete seriousness, a weight in every word. "To get you out of that situation."

"Hold on. You think I had anything to do with those black outs? The earthquake? You can't be serious. Those incidents weren't related to me at all. I was just in the wrong place at the wrong time."

"All right, then tell me a time that the power went off when you weren't panicked."

Okay. A time that the power went off when she wasn't panicked. The fact that she couldn't think of a single time, that didn't mean anything. There had to be one. She reached into her pockets for her lucky charm, her fingers seeking out the soft textures that would soothe away the thoughts racing through her. Her pockets were empty. It must have fallen out during the kidnapping, or it was lost at the bottom of the lake. She couldn't think of a time when there was an accident around her and she wasn't panicked. Not one. But that didn't mean what he suggested. She was unlucky, that was all it meant. Right?

Jun's heart started beating faster, and she hugged her arms tight against her chest to stop their shaking. There had to be a time. She just couldn't think right now. Trapped here, with the man who tried to kill her, being forced to think over the worst things ever to happen in her life, of course she was having trouble thinking calmly. Just because she couldn't come up with anything right on the spot didn't mean that it didn't happen.

Nikolai kicked dirt over the remnants of the fire, putting it out. He seemed to have reached a conclusion when she was unable to answer him. Now he stalked closer.

No. She was going to answer. She just needed more time to think it over.

"That earthquake wasn't the first time people have gotten hurt around you."

Jun shook her head. "You're wrong. That wasn't me. And even so, I wouldn't want to hurt anyone."

"But you have." He said it with such conviction that Jun ducked her head, unable to deny him. It was as if he could see inside her head and know the truth, but he couldn't have known about... about *her*.

Jun couldn't keep an image out of her head. The image of a hauntingly beautiful woman, willow thin and radiant. Someone she would never meet. Someone who only existed in photos, because of her.

She just needed more time. More time to think. More time to figure out exactly what was going on. More time to get away. Her throat was tight, closing up.

"Jun." Nikolai reached out for her, and he was going to do something to hurt her again. No. She was answering his questions. She was cooperating. Why couldn't he see that? This couldn't be happening. She couldn't think. She couldn't slow down her racing heart. She couldn't slow down her breaths or the burn at her eyes. She couldn't slow down the hand that cut across the distance between them.

No. Please. She needed just a little more time.

Nikolai's calloused hand pressed against her shoulder and it happened.

A sharp pulse of electricity spiraled between them at the touch of his skin against hers. It crackled within them and radiated outwards in a wave.

Nikolai's hand dropped away from her instantly like he was burned. He took a few steps away, keeping his distance, and for the first time he looked uncertain as he observed their surroundings. The silence was all around them until he spoke.

"What did you do?"

9

6 :53 a.m.

HE FELT IT AGAIN, A SURGE OF ENERGY WHEN HE TOUCHED her. It was obvious that she was on the verge of panic, and when he reached out to calm her down, the magic reacted, just as it had the first time when her thumb brushed against his palm and a current of wild, unnatural energy sparked against his skin. But this time it was stronger.

Nikolai waited for the ground to shift or for something to strike him down. Nothing happened.

"What did you do?" In the surreal silence around them, his voice carried. Not even the insects made a sound.

"I-I didn't do anything."

Nikolai took one look at her shaking hands and looked away. Maybe it had been a fluke, but his instincts told him otherwise. Something wasn't right. It was as if the very forest held its breath, watching.

Of course, the only thing to do now would be to kill her,

now that he was sure she was the magician. He hadn't needed to second-guess himself and take her all the way out into the woods. He hadn't needed to test her or to question her. If he wanted to do this right, play by all the rules, he would have pulled Jun into his apartment and finished her off. Before she could have a moment to retaliate.

If he had just let her drown then he wouldn't be in this mess.

Except he didn't have it in him when he saw her body drifting through murky waters. How her lips had turned blue, parted in a gasp.

He hadn't stopped to think. Not when he was swimming with her to the shore, and not when he was tilting back her chin, pinching her nose and breathing—forcing her chest to rise, forcing color back into her lips, forcing life back into her.

When her eyelids fluttered and she vomited out the water that was poisoning her, Nikolai felt like he too could breathe again.

Had he gotten it wrong? Was she just a civilian? He'd almost killed an innocent—something he vowed he'd never do. He'd misjudged something, but what?

No. He wasn't wrong. He'd seen hands shaking like Jun's too many times before. He must have lost his edge.

The sky should have been bright with dawn, but the light was barely passing through the leaves. Something had gone terribly wrong. But he'd already screwed this all up; he couldn't afford to be hasty. They couldn't just stay in the forest without any proper supplies, nor did it make sense to do something that he might regret later.

Pale and hunched into herself, Jun's lip was faintly trembling. She looked about as dangerous as a newborn kitten. He'd leave it for now.

"Come on, we're going."

"Going home?"

There was never going to be a going home for her. Not as long as the others were still out looking for the magician. "Yeah," he lied, so that she would follow.

It was a straight shot back to the road where the old car was still parked. It was no longer smoking.

Worth a shot to try it. Nikolai grasped the door handle and pulled without thinking. The handle wouldn't budge. Was the door locked? No. He could see that it was unlocked through the window. It was as if the entire thing was frozen solid—though it wasn't cold.

"What the hell." Nikolai braced his other hand against the door and yanked as if he was deadlifting six-hundred pounds, rather than trying to open a car door. Slowly, he could feel the mechanism unlatch.

"What, did my car freeze solid overnight?" Jun asked, watching from where she leaned against the guardrail.

"No. But you must have done something earlier in the woods." She didn't respond. Soundlessly, the door inched its way open, though Nikolai was still straining against it hard enough to rip it off its hinges. When he forced just enough space, Nikolai slipped through. He twisted the key where he left it in the ignition—or tried to. There wasn't enough leverage in the tight space with his palm twisted at an awkward angle. Fine. This was too much effort for a car that was probably still dead anyway.

"No good," he said.

In the passenger seat, he saw something that at first looked like some sort of plaid teddy bear. When he saw the straps, he vaguely recalled Jun with it in class. Figures she would be the kind of girl with a bear bag. He grabbed it, then yanked. At first the bag felt like it was over a hundred pounds, but as it lifted in the air closer to him it felt lighter. Nikolai paused, gauging the weight. Now it couldn't be any more than thirteen pounds or so. This wasn't like any kind of magic he had encountered before.

Nikolai wordlessly handed the bag over to her. "Do you have a phone?"

She shook her head. "It dropped and smashed when you kidnapped me."

"Oh." He didn't know quite what to say to that. "Sorry." He put his hands in his pockets uselessly. His phone lay somewhere at the bottom of the lake. Not that it mattered that it fell from his pocket, since he hadn't bothered with a waterproof case in the first place.

"Looks like we're walking."

"All the way back?"

"There's a gas station three miles down. We can see if there's a payphone. Or maybe we can hitch a ride."

She didn't look thrilled about either option, but then again, he couldn't blame her. In her own words, this was a kidnapping, but she had no idea how much she was a danger to others.

Nikolai started down the path and had to slow down since Jun was lagging behind. Nikolai looked her over for any lingering signs of weakness from the near drowning and noticed that she tensed up under his gaze.

It was going to be a long three miles.

It only took a few minutes for the silence to put him on edge. There was something jarring about the way that each footfall echoed into the distance. Dawn had yet to ease up, with the light streaming in at an angle. It should already be into early morning by now. The forest should be alive with bird calls, but there was only dead silence.

At a bend ahead, a car was stopped on the road, headlights shining their way. Nikolai approached the driver's side, ready to knock on the window, but stopped. At first, he thought the driver was having a stroke since he was staring blankly ahead, his face devoid of any expression. He wasn't moving at all, just kept a hand on the wheel and the other on the stick shift.

"No way." Jun muttered.

When he looked back, Jun was pointing toward the speedometer. The needle was pointing at 60. He blinked at the impossibility of what he was seeing. The car and man were completely immobile— frozen in space.

Then it clicked in his mind: the silence and stillness around them. Now that he knew, it was completely obvious. He looked back at Jun, whose face was in shadow, staring at the dashboard in confusion. It wasn't the car that was stuck, but them.

"Do you see it now?" Nikolai asked. "What you did?" There was no way she could deny magic now.

"How could any of this be real?" Her eyes widened when she finally looked back at him. "Oh... I'm dead. Oh, God. I'm dead. I drowned in the lake. None of this is real because you killed me."

Nikolai sighed. Just what had he gotten himself into? "Or," he said slowly, "you used magic and stopped time."

"This is crazy. I need to wake up." She pinched her arm and dragged a hand over face. "Come on, wake up."

"You're already awake. What you need to do is reverse this."

"Oh, yeah? And how would I do that?"

"I don't know, you're the magician. We're stuck like this until the magic wears off or you do something."

She shook her head and mumbled something under her breath, but otherwise remained quiet. They continued along the road, and no matter how far they went, nothing changed. Their pace was slow. Nikolai could have run the distance easily, but he made sure to keep close.

His stomach growled. Time may have stopped, but that didn't mean his appetite had as well. The last meal he had had was the day before, and though he could go for much longer without eating, he never liked to.

His training hadn't prepared him for this, but it did prepare him for the worst. One thing was clear—he couldn't kill her now and risk getting left behind in whatever haze of magic Jun had created. The thought made him pause. What if she left him here? Would he even be able to get out of this without her? Or would time go back to normal if she died? The risk was too great to chance it.

The trees began to thin out, and a gas station sign shined brightly in the distance. From here he could see the small convenience store and a car getting gas. As they got closer, it became apparent that the man at the pump was still. Not even his chest was moving to breathe. Through the window in the store was another man behind the register, staring blankly in space with his arm resting on the counter.

Nikolai ducked under the arm of a man frozen in the act of opening the door, and he couldn't quite avert his eyes from the frozen yawn etched on his face. It reminded him of a photograph, except that it was three dimensional, and he could feel the brush of warmth as he passed.

Nikolai stepped over to a container of Slim Jims, yanking out a handful. Again, he found that it was heavy until he pulled it closer to his body. He ripped off the plastic with his teeth, and in moments was replenishing calories, salt and proteins. He paused mid bite, wondering if there were any consequences to eating food tainted by magic. Maybe. But did he want to starve or deal with the consequences of magic-tainted food? He was already stuck. This Slim Jim was probably the least of his problems. Might as well not face it on an empty stomach.

He collected a few power bars, a pack of almonds, a red Gatorade, and an overly glazed Danish that he put in a plastic bag. At the back of the store, Jun gazed through the glass doors of the freezer. As she tugged on the handle, Nikolai half expected another show of magic—that the objects would somehow comply with her demands and spring open for her. Instead, Jun struggled half-heartedly at it with nothing to show for her efforts.

She stepped aside when he grabbed the handle. Again, he needed both of his hands as he pulled. Nothing happened the first five seconds, but then it started to give, until it suddenly wrenched all the way open, cracking like the glass would shatter any moment. He left it open, reaching his hand through the sudden wall of cold air. He grabbed the cup of Greek yogurt with honey and a side of granola that Jun had been eyeing and handed it to her once it began to feel less like a bowling ball.

"Anything else?"

Jun shook her head, frowning at the shattered glass held perfectly still in front of them.

From a side pocket, he pulled out two twenty-dollar bills. It would be too much effort to pry open the register, but he could lay the bill on the counter in front of the man staring at the cell phone in his lap. "Breakfast is on me."

"Charming."

He didn't quite get what was charming about it. He wasn't about to go on a stealing spree just because they could. Nor was he doing this because he particularly cared if she ate enough or not, especially now that he had proved that she was the magician. He just had to wait for time to

return to normal before killing her. This was about prac-
ticality.

Outside were a row of run-down benches with the white
paint peeling from the wood. It creaked when Nikolai sat
down on the one closest to the door. Immediately, he started
on a power bar.

Jun choose a seat further down. Her hands shook as she
tugged against the plastic seal on her yogurt, and she only
managed opening it after she clenched her hands and
fought with the lid.

*There's no way that she's pretending that she can barely open
a yogurt container.*

Every magician he had ever seen was a monster. They
clearly needed to be put down before they turned on civil-
ians. Not looking up at him like a baby harbor seal, while he
was the fur trader with the club.

Was it possible? Did she really have no idea what she
was capable of?

He would just have to watch her until she became
dangerous like the rest of them.

10

Hanging immobile in the purple and orange sky was the unmistakable silhouette of an airplane against a cream-colored cloud. On the road in front of them were silent cars. No engines rumbling, no tires crunching loose asphalt, no squeaking brakes. Just pairs of headlights illuminating the early morning gloom—though it shouldn't be early morning anymore. If the rumbling in Jun's stomach was any indication, it was well past the afternoon.

She unashamedly looked into each car.

The time on the dashboards glowed 6:53, the moment when time stopped. Some of the drivers had their hands fixed onto the steering wheel and looked resolutely ahead of them, but not all. The man in the beamer had his hand wrapped around a gas station breakfast burrito with his mouth open wide for his first bite. The driver of the brand new Tesla was looking down at his lap, in the middle of a text message that read: *Miss having you in my b.*

Had she caused this?

Jun had always known that she was unlucky. Was it really so strange to think that she could have caused something? If misfortune was going to happen to anyone, it might as well happen to her. Made sense that she would get the talent that brought a bunch of bloodthirsty assholes to her front door.

A rustle. Something brushing against the leaves.

What was that?

Jun stopped to listen. It hadn't come from any of the bushes or trees that she could see; everything was as eerily quiet and still as it had been since the world stopped.

"What is it?" Nikolai asked from ahead.

She shook her head and began to walk again. "It's nothing."

It felt like hours before they took an exit off the highway to reach the next convenience store. As they approached the neon green and orange lights of the 7-Eleven gas station, Nikolai's stomach grumbled loudly. Huh. It was good to know that she wasn't the only one running on empty.

It wasn't until they were close enough to see through the glass doors and the cashier frozen in the act of restocking coffee creamer that they realized the problem—the doors were shut.

There was no groove that Nikolai could grasp to force the automatic doors open. He ran his fingers against the metal seam, looking for a place to get a grip, before cursing.

Inside this 7-Eleven there was a cold sandwich display, and it was a mark of how hungry she was that Jun couldn't tear her eyes away from it.

"I wonder how long it's been," she said aloud, not really expecting an answer. They hadn't talked much since the last gas station.

"We're walking at an average pace, so about three miles an hour, and the sign on the highway said fifteen miles to the next rest stop. So I'd say roughly five or six hours since we last ate."

Fifteen miles? No wonder her feet felt like they wanted to fall off. She could already feel fat blisters forming on her toes.

"Do you know how long it is to the next stop?"

"I didn't see a sign." Nikolai stepped back and looked around.

"Now what? It's not like we can wait for it to open."

He went around back, and Jun followed a few paces behind into a cramped space between two buildings. Of course there was no back entrance, only a dumpster and folded up cardboard boxes lined the wall. The dumpster reeked. Nikolai reached for the lid. He wasn't seriously going to go dumpster diving, was he? Jun was hungry, but she wasn't past that point of starving. Thankfully, he only pulled himself on top of it. Then he lowered a hand for her to follow.

Looking up, Jun understood. There was an escape ladder within reaching distance from the dumpster across from them. Two stories up was an open window. "You're not serious?"

"Would you rather walk six more hours back to the last gas station?"

Jun took his hand.

Effortlessly, he pulled her up. She wouldn't have been able to reach the metal ladder if he hadn't lifted her onto that, either. There was a faint smell of cigarette smoke. The rusted metal creaked under their weight. She ducked, easing her way inside when she saw the man facing her with a cigarette in hand. She started and raked her back hard against the wooden frame.

"Ow, damn it." Jun rubbed the tender area along her spine.

"What is it?" Nikolai asked, and when he leaned closer to see, he smirked. "Really? What's so scary about this guy?"

Nothing now that she knew that he was there. Jun frowned. "Did you even look at his mustache? It's big enough to crawl off his face and come after us."

His eyebrow lifted, and then he slowly shook his head. "If that's all, then I'm heading in."

Jun followed after him. It took a few moments for her eyes to adjust to the darkness and make out the living room. It was cramped, with dirty dishes, wadded napkins and mail strewn across every surface. The only shred of color was the faded burgundy couch that looked like it was as old as the apartment. Tucked in the corner was a TV, the glow of the screen advertising the price of an industrial strength vacuum.

There was an adjoining kitchen where Nikolai was already scavenging. He wrenched the yellowing cabinets open.

"This is depressing." Nikolai closed one cabinet and started on another. "The guy is living off cans and microwave meals."

Three slices of white bread were left in a bag. Jun grappled with the plastic, the tension slow to give way before breaking free.

Nikolai put what he could find on the table—pickle jars, tuna cans, noodle packets, diet Pepsi and the frozen meals he'd managed to take out from the nearly empty refrigerator.

Jun searched through the piles of stuff for a clean plate, going so far as brushing off awkward crumbs, before giving up and placing the bread on top of a napkin. Her hands flicked over the different options. Should she have a sad bologna or sad tuna sandwich? Was the bologna green in that corner? All right, sad tuna it was.

She opened the can and dumped a glob of gray fish mush onto the stale bread. She was hungry enough that her creation actually looked appetizing. There were no chairs, so Jun carried it over to the sofa and began to eat, feeling human again after the first couple of bites.

Plastic crinkled and then she heard a crunch. Nikolai, from where he sat on the counter, ate a dried-out square of noodles.

Jun polished off the sandwich and tried to sink deeper into the stiff cushions. She should probably get up and scrounge around for something else. She closed her eyes, just for a second. Just to think through the options and figure out what to eat.

Jun took a deep breath and rubbed her eyes, confused for a moment. Her neck was sore the way she was resting against the arm of the sofa, the metal and wood poking through the coarse material. She hadn't meant to fall asleep. Jun turned over in hopes to dream silently once more. It was much better than facing what her reality had become. Magic was still more like an absurd dream. All she wanted was to get back home with her comfortable knitted blankets so she could finish her degree. Was that too much to ask for? She didn't need any of this right now. There was the final in a month, and then she could graduate.

She would never have found herself waking up here, mouth dry and tasting of canned fish and preservatives, if it wasn't for him. Snoring traveled from across the room. Jun craned her neck to see Nikolai slumped against the counter, exhausted. Jun came up with the perfect snarky comment, regarding the hard work kidnapping must be, when she froze.

He was asleep.

Slowly, Jun shifted forward, keeping her weight on the balls of her feet. She eased off the couch with a faint creak, then padded over to the window, slinging her bag across her back as she went. From here it was a very long drop from the escape ladder to the ground below. It wouldn't take much of a margin of error for her to end up with a broken leg. Or worse. Jun clenched her grip on the ledge as the view down below made her dizzy.

Was it safer to stay? Was it safe for Jun to stick around and see whether or not Nikolai was going to kill her in the near future?

Jun gripped the metal tight. All she had to do was not look down. Just don't look down. She could do this.

That thought worked with her first step, and even with the second and third. All the way until she reached the last rung of the ladder and clutched hard to the metal rungs as her foot met air. She nearly lost her footing completely.

The drop down was taller than she was. She carefully lowered herself until she was only hanging on by her hands before dropping to the ground. Her ankles felt the shock, pain shooting up to her knees, and she fell sideways to catch herself. Jun stayed like that, her eyes immediately going back to the window and expecting to see Nikolai any second. Seeing nothing, she moved, ignoring the scrapes along her palms and knees. When she was out of the alley, she ran.

11

A rough vibration like a garbage truck by his ear jostled Nikolai awake. He hadn't meant to fall asleep, hadn't even realized he had done it.

He rubbed his hand down his face to force himself to wake up. How was Jun so loud? What was she doing? Last he had seen of her, she'd taken just a few bites before passing out. That girl needed more calories in her. With twenty miles to go through steep California hills, she'd soon feel depleted without an energy boost. But she was picky about food. Nikolai frowned and slipped off the counter. She wasn't on the sofa—not anywhere in the cluttered living room.

He crossed the room, scanning over the rickety furnishing. "Jun?"

He turned back and knocked on the partially open bathroom. "Hey, you in there?" When no response came, he peered in and found the empty toilet mocking him.

What the hell? She wasn't anywhere in the house. Where could she have gone…

Oh *fuck.*

Nikolai swallowed hard and went to the window. No sign of her outside. He climbed down the fire escape and tried reading the ground for clues on which direction she'd headed. There were no secrets spilled on the dirty pavement.

He took off running, heading back toward her campus. He doubted she'd go the other way. Nothing was usable or familiar to her in the arid countryside. For three miles he charged down the highway, weaving around frozen cars— the only sound was the grating of his own breath. He had to catch up, couldn't fall any more behind.

After another mile with no sign of her, he slowed to a stop, breathing hard. This was useless. She could be anywhere. That was, if she was even still here to be found. What about that noise that had woken him up? Could that have been her magic as she left? What if he was stuck here forever? He crushed the rising panic in its tracks.

He was an assassin, not an idiot. He had been trained to handle the worst. Nikolai unclenched his jaws and took a deep breath, easing the headache pounding in his ears.

She'd hide out somewhere familiar to her. But where was familiar?

He memorized entire life histories for those in the class deemed suspicious. But her? She'd been overlooked. With time stopped, it wasn't as if he could research Jun.

But then again, why not? Obviously, he wouldn't be able to access electronic data, but hard files? There had to be records of Jun at the university or the pizza joint.

Nikolai broke out in a brisk jog that he could hold for miles. The entire time he looked out for Jun or clues to where she could have gone. It must have been hours before his luck turned and he spotted a bike.

A man in a cowboy hat was stopped in the process of

opening a garage door. Behind him was a racing bike, covered in dust and cobwebs.

"Sorry about the bike," Nikolai said as he passed the man and ducked into the garage. Clear tubs lined the wall. In one there was a box with Capri Sun and pretzels. "And the food," Nikolai added as he forced open the flimsy lid that now felt like it had been sealed with wet cement. He lined his pockets with pouches and pretzel packets.

At first the pedals wouldn't give an inch, but after some forceful kicks, they shifted and broke free. The chain was rusty and the gears didn't work, but the bike lifted his mood. The absence of time flew by. He passed through towns, crisscrossing between cars as he went. It was impossible to tell just how long he biked, but when he finally made it to the pizza place, his legs burned from exhaustion.

Feelin' Saucy was closed, the doors and windows shut. His only option was to break in. Nikolai hurled a rock a dozen times before the window cracked, then shattered all at once. Mindful of fingerprints, he wore gloves—though he wasn't sure if traces of his activities would remain once time restarted. Luckily his gloves hadn't fallen out when he'd saved Jun from drowning. Nikolai avoided the loose glass as he lifted himself through the ledge and stepped into the dark space.

The aroma of stale pizza greeted him, and his mouth watered. Behind the counter, a small drawer looked promising. Tricky—not much purchase on the thin wooden panel. But Nikolai wrenched it open with brute force. Inside were paper records of the employees, including Jun Bear's resume. Complete with her current address at the campus.

After memorizing the important information, he folded up the paper several times and tucked it away in his jacket. He turned, ready to leave, when his stomach growled.

In the back, he found a mini fridge. One quick tug like he was grabbing a fifty-pound free weight and it was open.

Bingo—grease-stained plates held slices of the best pizza in town. Flavors hit him in a rush. Even cold and with grease that stuck to the back of his throat, this was heaven. With two more slices stacked together, Nikolai sat on the desk and continued to eat. He was mentally mapping the fastest route to campus when a low rumble like slowed down rotations of helicopter blades cut through the silence.

Nikolai dropped the slices and turned, knife in hand.

The sound was loudest in the back corner of the room, behind a closet door. Nikolai shifted his hold on the blade to a pinch grip as an unsettling chill filled the air. He wasn't alone.

There was something in the closet.

He crept closer.

The air hummed with static energy, all tinged with the scent of burnt ozone.

Creaking, the door slid open all on its own. Slowly, it swung wide, until the wood thudded against the wall. Inside was nothing but black shadows.

Something shifted in the darkness.

Nikolai hurled his knife into the closet. As the blade hit plaster, the rumbling stopped. Once again, it was quiet and still.

Nikolai retrieved the knife, yanking it free. Cracks grew, spreading outwards from the point where the blade struck, and slowly spread along the walls like fracturing ice. Within the cracks were shadows, too dark to be natural.

The wall splintered and broke apart in a web, surrounding him. Nikolai raced for the exit, jumping over breaks along the floor. A deep chasm cut Nikolai off from the entrance, trapping him. He made a dash for the window, reaching it just as chinks fractured into the windowsill. When he touched the ledge to jump over, pain seared across his gloved hand.

He dove for the bike and peddled like mad, his hurt palm an afterthought. The crap bike was nearly impossible to control with one hand. Twice he scraped against a car door. It wasn't until he was five blocks away that he checked his hand.

He tugged the glove a few times before it peeled off. His skin had blackened in jagged lines, matching the cracks he had touched in the window ledge. He had some movement in his fingers, but the black areas were unnaturally stiff, as if half of his hand was stopped in time. It took an enormous effort to twitch the blackened flesh. His grip was shot, too.

Nikolai gritted his teeth, pounding his good fist on the bike's handlebar. What the hell was that thing? Obviously magic, but there was no magician in sight. Whatever it was, it had taken out his non-dominant hand. Leaving him crippled, but not defenseless.

He hurried on to the campus dorms, accompanied by the constant squeaking of the bike.

Halfway there and running on empty, Nikolai hit the curb, and the rusted front wheel popped off the bike. The whole thing tipped forward, and the momentum took Nikolai down. He hit the asphalt hard, the force jarring and unexpected.

Where his sleeves were rolled up, Nikolai's skin was scraped raw. Except for one area. The black mark on his hand was pristine. Untouched. Nikolai brushed off the dirt and debris from the wound. He tore off his sleeve, ripping it into makeshift bandages to cover the worst of it. Could he get an infection? Or were the bacteria frozen in time too? At any rate, that was all he could do for now.

Nikolai returned to the road to jog the rest of the way.

By the time he found the right dorm building, Nikolai lost all sense of time. Exhausted, his body was worn out. Had he last slept twenty-four hours ago? He had no way to tell.

Nikolai picked at the dorm lock, but he couldn't exert the right pressure in its frozen state. Instead he circled the dorms, peering into the windows to find a hint of the room numbers.

There. On the first floor. He saw the placard with the number II on the backside of the door and grinned. Nikolai's gaze swept the ground around him. He stopped to pick up a rock but dropped it almost immediately, cursing. He'd automatically grabbed it with his non-dominant hand. His thumb and pointer were so unwieldy they might as well have been dead.

Subtlety be damned, Nikolai bashed through the once pristine bay windows of Jun's dormitory. The glass cracked and hung upright in a broken web. Nikolai pressed with his full body weight to topple it to the ground.

Neither the redhead typing at her computer nor the sleeping pimply kid were Jun. Damn it. Nikolai peered closer at the placard on the far door. 17, not II. A lamp had obscured the top of the number from his view outside.

He smashed apart the correct windows to find she wasn't in her dorm room—not that he really expected her to be. The side that was covered in fluffy knitted shit was empty. The other sported some girl with her mouth frozen open, with a faint trickle of drool dampening the bedding by her mouth.

He went by Jun's desk first. There were folders arranged by color, a closed laptop, and a picture of a fluffy rodent with a top hat. In the desk drawers were knitting crafts and spools of wool. He dug through yarn balls in every shade of the pastel rainbow. More than she needed if the knitting was a deliberate way to fade into the background as some innocent wallflower. No. Jun must actually like this shit. Underneath a set of gel pens were cards, letters, and photos. He went through the photos first. The only people in them were her and an old guy that had to be her father. The rest of the photos were of that rodent again. He checked the cards. The one on top was a birthday card from her father. The envelope was addressed, and Nikolai put that one in his pocket.

As he went through her closet, with its empty suitcase and stacks of old textbooks and folders, he heard it again—a guttural snarl. Deep. Slowed down, promising violence.

Nikolai unsheathed his knife. The sound was above, coming from shadows in the dark. He shifted to a hammer grip when the sound ceased. Nikolai paused for a half a breath. He turned and ran out the room, jumping through the broken window.

A blast surged behind him in an icy wave. His eardrums popped, filling his head with a sharp ringing. He collapsed onto the school lawn, surrounded by bits of yarn and wood fragments the same color as Jun's desk.

Nikolai got up, ready to run, fully expecting something to be following him. But everything in Jun's room was unmoving. Not a single sign to show something out of the ordinary, other than Jun's broken things left scattered on the lawn.

Even so, Nikolai was sure it was still there, watching him. Whatever it was, it obviously wanted him dead.

12

J un's hands flicked between the almond croissant and the hard-boiled eggs. The croissants here were *divine,* but she had already had twelve of them, at least two for each meal since she had arrived. What was she going to do when she got sick of them? But then again, was it even possible to get sick of a pastry with such a delicate flaky crust? Jun grabbed the croissant, adding it to the pear and green apple already on her plate.

"Excuse me." She stepped around the hotel attendant, who was frozen in the act of adding bacon to the platter. "The food here is absolutely fabulous. Keep up the good work."

Jun crossed the hallway, marveling at the geometric print on the carpets, until she reached a row of doorways. "Thanks again for letting me borrow the place," Jun said to a middle-aged woman in a business suit, frozen in the act of staring worriedly at her watch as she stepped out of the room. Jun slipped around her. She settled cross legged on the second queen-sized bed—the room had two, and this one was untouched. She had to come to this place again; the thread count on these sheets was higher than her annual salary at Feelin' Saucy.

The croissant was perfect. Just the right blend of buttery pastry with a good hint of almond. She looked out the window at the dark outline of palm trees in a glorious pink and orange sunrise. The same sunrise she had admired... for how long? Had it been just a couple days? Had it been a week already? It made no difference. Same delicious croissant. Same comfortable bed. The hotel was the loveliest cage she had ever been in. Almost lovely enough to forget that she was trapped. She could walk home, and she would never be home. Her entire life was frozen, and she was stuck outside of it.

She would stay here for the rest of her life. Then someday that lovely hotel attendant restocking the bacon would come back to this room and find Jun's old-aged, dried out corpse as she was trapped out of the rest of her life.

This was ridiculous. There was no such thing as stopped time. Jun tossed her plate in the air and caught it. The repetitive motion as she continued to throw it was soothing.

She had to be in a coma or something. She must have drowned in the lake and now she was in a coma waiting to wake up. Or maybe she'd had a mental breakdown from stress and made all of this up. Things like this didn't just happen. Like magic.

Deny it all you want. You're never getting out of here.

Jun sighed. Why did that sound suspiciously like Suzie? She shouldn't be going crazy yet; it couldn't have been more than a week. She wasn't lonely or anything, especially not for Suzie's company. By now she should be used to being by herself. But it was boring. There wasn't much to do here besides eat and sleep, and Jun had already explored every accessible space in the hotel, which meant she had walked down the hall, front desk, and cafeteria fifty times now. Of course her brain would be making unpleasant conversation.

"It's not like I'm going crazy," she told the reflection of herself in the TV, not the TV itself. Or maybe it would be better to be crazy than the whole magic thing. It would make more logical sense. Jun shimmied further onto the bed so her legs weren't dangling off the mattress. She continued to toss the plate and catch it.

What she really needed right now was her knitting set, then she could pretend this was an overdue vacation and not the endless nightmare that it was. There was always the option of finding a craft store, but even if she found one, it would be forever closed, and it didn't sit right with her to break in when it had been her dream to own one since she was seven and first learned to cross stitch a scarf for her dad. He'd been so happy—she knew right away she'd continue making things and eventually help others do the same. But that was all over. Forget her dream. Forget seeing her dad again.

"This is all his fault." If Nikolai hadn't kidnapped her. If he hadn't driven her to the middle of nowhere. If he hadn't thrown her into the water, none of this would have happened. She would be back having sushi with her dad, then wrapping up her last semester of college.

Jun flung herself back onto the ridiculously comfortable bed, her grip on the plate tight enough to hurt.

No. A thought nagged at her. You know that it wasn't him. You know that's not true. It hadn't been Nikolai who had stopped time.

She was about to fling the plate in the air when something in the design caught her attention. The engraved floral pattern that rimmed the plate had a rabbit nibbling a flower, and Jun was a hundred percent positive that rabbit wasn't there before.

There was something familiar about it, even though there shouldn't have been. It wasn't like she had ever had a pet rabbit before. Something about the shape of it nagged at her.

She brought the plate closer to examine it and blinked. It was a little white rabbit, but it wasn't eating a flower anymore. It was staring right back at her.

Jun shrieked and hurled the plate away, and it shattered against the wall. The broken shards fell to the lush carpet, where they lay in silent accusation. It took a full minute before her pulse settled and she told herself she was being dumb. It was only a plate. All this 'magic' nonsense was scaring her into thinking she was seeing things.

Still, she hesitated before heading over to clean the mess. It wasn't like room service was going to come anytime soon and do it for her.

She knelt down, picking up the broken pieces one by one, frowning. Where was it? She checked under the bed, but she had gotten all of the plate shards. Muttering to herself that this was stupid, Jun began arranging the broken pieces on the carpet, looking for it. But it was clear that the rabbit was no longer there. It was gone. Poof. Like magic.

But there's no such thing as magic.

Jun looked again at the woman in the business suit. Her eyes were slanted down, open. Jun knew from squeezing past her that her skin was warm, despite the stillness.

Why bother to deny it?

She had done this. Denying what she'd done wasn't

going to get her out of this mess, but maybe believing that there was magic would do something. Make time start up again. It would make more sense if magic was real.

"Magic is real," she muttered to herself. She looked at the plate to see if it changed, but it had not. Jun squeezed her eyes shut, her hands equally tight. "Magic is real." She said it three more times before stopping and chuckling at her antics. Nothing happened; not a single particle of dust suspended in air shifted. "Yeah, like that's going to work."

She went back to the bed and flopped down on the covers, suddenly exhausted with it all. Closing her eyes, she thought taking a nap would straighten her out. The blankets were still tucked under the mattress as they had been when Jun had arrived. The past couple of nights, the temperature had remained steady and she hadn't needed them. But a sudden chill wracked her body now, and Jun made the effort to get under the blankets.

Her eyelids were heavy and her breathing was evening out when she first felt something was off. She was cold. The temperature around her was rapidly descending. When she tried to move, Jun found her limbs stiff. Her fingers trembled as she tried to force herself up, but she was frozen in place. The only motion in the room were her rapid breaths condensing into a fog.

This was a dream, right? She was sleeping and had to wake up. But how could she be sleeping when she had never fallen asleep in the first place? Even blinking became difficult. Her eyelids were weighted, hardening in place. Wide-eyed, Jun scanned the room—for what, she didn't know.

This was worse than sleep paralysis. What if she became frozen like the objects in the room, forever stuck in time? If she didn't move now, the magic would catch her. If she didn't—wait, what was that?

She thought she had heard something, a scratching noise. Her breathing was shallow and fast, too loud in the silence, and Jun tried to suck in the frigid air quietly.

It came again, a faraway noise creaking along the plaster ceiling, thudding against the carpet floors above her hotel room in a rhythmic pattern like footsteps. But it couldn't be. Nothing here moved, not since time stopped. Everything else was still and silent. But the noise of it was stark against the silence.

Jun was immobile and powerless. Her limbs twitched in her desperation to escape. The noise seemed to stop, a passing foreboding, before the scratching came again, hollow and heavy inside of the closet door. She was facing it directly, her vision watered from the force of trying to jerk her head away, trying to move any part of herself. It was the same closet that she tried to open once before and knew for a fact was stuck like everything else.

Jun couldn't just lie there. Not with something right behind the closet door. Telling herself that she had to move did nothing against the cold that held her. Her nails dug into her flesh as she clenched down on every muscle and wrenched upwards, trying to force herself away. Her vision blurred with the strain. Her body jolted an inch to the left, still and stiff.

She gulped down the air in deep breaths. Worn out, she hadn't even managed to turn away from her view of the closet. The doorknob creaked as it began to twist.

It was coming for her; it would kill her if it could. Even separated by the flimsy panel of wood, the desire to maim, to destroy, was a thick smog in the air. Her limbs were locked up, her strength nothing against the overwhelming pressure anchoring her down, but Jun didn't want that thing anywhere near her. She had been kidnapped, drowned, thrown into this surreal world—she wasn't going to die here, lying passively in a hotel room. Her father wouldn't survive the shock if he turned on the TV and saw the news about her mysterious death. She had to move; she needed to move.

Beads of sweat began to form along her back from the exertion. A sudden heat flooded through her veins, growing hotter and hotter until it felt like it would burst from her skin. At last she could blink and look away.

The doorknob clicked, a sound like ice cracking.

With a heave, Jun toppled out of bed, the impact traveling through her stiff limbs and loosening her further. Her only exit was past the closet, and Jun did not hesitate as she crawled forward and dragged her heavy limbs.

When the door creaked open, dark, smoke-like tendrils writhed in the gap as more pushed through to force it open. Jun dragged herself to her feet, stumbling into a run. She collided into the business suit woman and uttered a hasty "sorry" as she ducked under the outstretched arm.

Warmth burned through her, churning through her muscles, urging her on. She ran, faster than she ever had, down the narrow corridor, followed by the sounds of wood creaking and snapping.

As she passed the hotel lobby, a small white rabbit was sitting in the free candy bowl before it scampered away, tipping the bowl of peppermints to the ground.

It wasn't until she was back on the highway, doubled over, her hands clutching the stitch in her side, when she finally had a moment to think. All right. Apparently in the stopped time there was some sort of evil presence that wanted to hunt her down. That should have been the strangest thing to happen to her, even with time stopping, the assassin, and the sort of date with Bailey. But that wasn't the thought nagging at her. She kept thinking back to the hotel lobby. No, that wasn't even the first time she had seen it.

Why was there a little white rabbit hopping around and following her?

13

The house was easily the smallest on the block, olive green with a purple door. It was overdue in repairs: paint chipping, loose roof tiles, and an overgrown lawn. Nikolai nearly kicked over a hidden gnome nestled between the roots of a peach tree as he crossed the yard, and there were more scattered along the tall grass, only their faded red hats visible.

So this was where Jun lived. It wasn't quite the evil lair Nikolai imagined a magician's home would look like, but then again Jun hadn't quite matched any of his expectations. As he circled the house, there were no easy entry points, and more importantly no sign that Jun had been here. Good, he could rest, then. He'd been on the road for so long, he'd lost all track of time. It could have been a week or more.

Without his phone's GPS, Nikolai had to hunt down a physical copy of a map—who had those anymore? Luckily, he'd spotted a map in the back of a classic Mercedes-Benz that now sported a broken window. It had taken so long that he'd pushed himself harder in case she beat him home.

His only rest had been the occasional park bench, though he slept with the threat of the creature stalking him. Any one place he stayed too long, he'd sense it. Feel the air charge. Hear the creaking of warping floors and walls. It was worse when he broke into stores or houses, as if it were waiting for him there. Nikolai stuck to the open roads as much as he could help it.

Now he'd found his destination—a house that was sure to draw her in. All he had to do was wait. He had all the time in the world to find her. That was, if she was still out there.

He circled the block, picking a vantage point with a clear view of Jun's house. It was a few houses down and across the street. The porch was well lit and had a comfortable hammock.

It must have been a few hours before he was unable to keep his eyes open. He settled into an uneasy pattern of sleeping, occasionally jerking awake, certain the thing was going to be after him. Or that he would miss something.

Each time he awoke, he would stare at the motionless scene of the stalled car backing out of the driveway, a man in a bathrobe walking his poodle, the bird flying to a nest close enough to touch if he reached out his hand. He'd watch the scenery, look down the road, and keep watch until either sleep or hunger took him.

The easiest available food was the unripe fruits from a neighbor's peach tree. As long as he stayed trapped like this, they would always be a few days away from ripening. He chewed the hard flesh of tart fruits, with nothing but the growing pile of discarded pits to mark the passing of time.

He had no idea how long he waited, but it was long enough to doubt if she was even going to come. What was worse than the wait, the growing uncertainty, and the sour taste of unripe peaches perpetually itching the back of his throat was the complete silence. It plagued his dreams. After the utter silence of being awake, his dreams were painfully loud. Often he was startled awake, jarred into a fight-or-flight response, from growls, screams and screeches ringing in his head.

The silence was oppressive—a tangible absence weighing down on him. Nikolai was used to being alone. On the hunt, researching, he'd spend hours and days alone. But there had always been others around, even if he chose not to speak to them. He hadn't realized how lonely it would be when that choice was taken away.

Getting here kept him distracted. Now, there was nothing to stand in the way of his isolation.

He was alone. Completely alone. Nothing but the sound of his own breaths kept him company.

Never to hear another human voice.

Never to see another smile.

Never to feel the warmth of soft skin.

Time went by—just for him. The rest of the world was locked away.

This is how you die. Heart's still beating. Lungs still breathing. Never escaping. You're already dead, you just don't know it. Nikolai shook his head, clearing the thoughts.

He stared down the same stretch of unmoving road as the stillness grated away at him, little by little. He didn't know how much more of it he could take.

When he first spotted movement, Nikolai was sure he was hallucinating. How could someone even tell if they were sane or not? But the movement—the first he'd seen in forever—was coming closer. That purple hat was unmistakable, vibrant when his memories of it had all but faded. Something his brain couldn't make up. He held his breath, reigning in the brimming euphoria at seeing another live person.

Adrenaline and a vibrant sense of weightlessness pumped through his veins. He'd found her. He wasn't left behind, trapped. He fought to control the feeling before he started grinning like an idiot.

Jun ambled down the road, swinging her arms, carefree. Her sleek, dark hair swayed behind her with each step. She was small and lithe. Closer, her doe-like eyes came into view —dark and lovely in a heart-shaped face.

Beautiful.

Nikolai's eyes widened as he tensed. He had to force himself to relax, to calm the rapid beating of his heart.

What the hell was that?

Jun was dangerous. Earthquakes. Stopping time. God only knew what else. She had no idea of what she could do, and no control of her magic. She could kill him or kill thousands of innocents. Easily.

This was a whole new level of idiotic. He really must have been losing his damn mind.

Jun tried the front door of her house, then went around to the side. When he could no longer see her, Nikolai moved.

Jun was struggling with the window, pushing against the unyielding wood panel in her attempt to break into her own house. It was ajar, but that window may as well have been nailed shut.

"I wouldn't." His voice was raw, strange to his own ears from how long it had been since he'd last used it. The rest of his sentence died in his throat.

Jun gasped and banged her elbow with how fast she turned around. "You—" she started to say, freezing with panic, before taking a step to run.

"Don't." Nikolai stepped in her path, blocking her off, then held his hands up and took a step back. "It's all right," he finished lamely.

"What are you doing here?" She narrowed her eyes, but something else occurred to her, and fear drained the color from her face. "What have you done to him?" Jun turned to look through the window anxiously. It dawned on him a moment later.

"I'm not here for him." Which was the wrong thing to say, as Jun visibly tensed. Shit. Calming down frightened women was definitely not part of his skill set. "Look, I don't want to hurt you, I just want to get out of here."

"You want me to help you?" Jun laughed in a way that had Nikolai imagining eating unripe peaches for the rest of his miserable life, at least until that thing caught up with him. "After everything you did? Why should I?"

"Because we could help each other." After searching for weeks, how had he managed to screw things up already? He'd thought about what he'd say to Jun, rehearsed this conversation dozens of times. Nothing was working out like it had in his head.

She gave him a pointed look over, from the top of his unwashed hair to the sweat-stained clothes he'd been wearing for at least a week's time. "I don't need your help. Besides, why should I help you? You tried to kill me."

"If I wanted to kill you, you'd be dead."

"Is that supposed to make me trust you? And yes, you did try to kill me. You dragged me out into the middle of nowhere and almost drowned me." Jun shuffled back, drawing away as she glared at him.

"I didn't just drag you out in the middle of nowhere." His voice was sore and felt raw, though anger fueled his words. "I took you away from others to stop you from hurting innocent bystanders. And I wasn't trying to drown you. I assumed that you were playing dumb. I thought that the water would trigger the magic out of you and then you'd go kick my ass."

"You're crazy if you think I'm going to be able to kick anyone's ass, especially yours. And throwing me in a lake because I'm so dangerous is an overreaction if I've ever seen one."

Nikolai's whole body tensed. Overreaction? "The magician I tracked down before you was especially creative in the way that he killed people. Turned parts of them inside out. Lit their organs on fire. Made people disappear into the floor."

Nikolai stared down at his hands. None of those people deserved to die. If anything, moving and reacting faster could have saved some of them. "The seventh magician I tracked liked to age people rapidly. He took whole decades away from his victims. The third magician I tracked started a tsunami that killed fifty thousand people."

Nikolai closed the space between them as his voice deepened. "And the first magician I saw killed my brother. Incinerated him into ashes right in front of me. So no, I don't think that I'm overreacting."

But Jun shook her head. "That can't be true. I've never heard of anything like that before."

"People will rationalize away anything to make it fit with what makes sense to them. Missing persons. Unnatural phenomenon. Magic. Just because you don't want to believe it doesn't make it untrue."

"If you really think I'm that dangerous, it doesn't make sense for me to free you up to kill me later." Jun crossed her arms. "I'll take my chances. Alone."

"Look, I don't hurt innocent people. As long as you aren't

going on some killing rampage, I promise that I won't do anything to hurt you."

She didn't look convinced.

"You came here because you wanted things to feel normal. You wanted to be someplace safe. If you want things to go back to normal, take my help."

Jun stared resolutely at the window, refusing to look at him. She didn't have a plan; otherwise she wouldn't be here, aimlessly wandering back home.

Nikolai sighed. Hell, what did he have to lose? He wrenched the window open, wide enough for her to go through.

Jun opened her mouth and closed it again, burying whatever question or comment she had for him. She eased up and into the window, hanging on the sill precariously, before disappearing into the dark depths of the house.

It wasn't a good idea. They didn't have that much time left before it came. What if it attacked Jun and he got stuck here forever? But he couldn't keep her around if he didn't gain her trust. It wasn't like he could stay awake forever, watching her. No, she would slip away in his sleep.

Nikolai backed away, crushing weeds and overgrown flowerbeds in his haste. He went as far as hopping over a neighbor's fence in case that thing really was after him only. There he waited, watching. Eyes trained on the frozen house, waiting for Jun to do what she needed to do. For her to get back out of there.

Once again, he stared at the house and waited.

It was distant and muffled, but in the silence, it might as well have been the retort of a pistol. The house was creaking. Was it too much to hope that Jun was fumbling around inside? There it was again, the groan of wood, as if the very floorboards were aching, pain reverberated down into the foundation, the structure of it. It was a noise that Nikolai had become too familiar with. Too angry to be natural. The thing was here.

Would going in make it worse?

Maybe. Maybe it would go easier on her. His heartbeat rang in his ears as the creaking became louder. He couldn't take that chance. If something happened to her, Nikolai would be left behind.

Nikolai flung himself over the fence and to the window. The tight fit of the wooden frame scraped his skin raw and ripped jagged lines down his shirt as he shoved himself through.

For a moment, Nikolai stopped to adjust to the dim light, finding he was in a sparse kitchen. On a scratched up square table was a bowl of oatmeal with steam spiraling up, and what looked like a ripe peach chopped up on a small cutting board. Standing in front of the sink was a wrinkled man, only a few inches over five feet, washing off a pot. He wore an apron with cartoon fish and rubber gloves.

If he was here, then where the hell was Jun?

The hallways were empty, and Nikolai didn't trust the blackness that bordered the shadows. The house was too small; there wasn't exactly space for her to hide. He passed by doors that were ajar, listening intently to the occasional creaking that couldn't be her. Scratches that didn't even sound human. Nikolai rushed past.

There was a door at the end of the hallway painted lilac, and the shadows at the wall's edge reached into it.

"Jun," he called out as loud as he dared.

She didn't reply.

Damn it. Right. Better to just go for it, then. Like a Band-Aid. Rip this shit right out and into the open.

Nikolai burst into the room, hands on the cool metal of his blade.

Jun was sitting in front of a cage that contained her fluffy pet rodent. She appeared to be trying to pry the wire door open with a set of knitting needles.

In the upper ceiling, tendrils of shadow reached for her like a many-armed spider.

Nikolai grabbed her and yanked her out of the way, just as clawed hands crashed down.

14

Something hard around Jun's stomach wrenched her back. There came a crunch of twisting metal as black tendrils tore into the cage, missing her. Jun craned her neck to see Nikolai behind her, his gaze locked toward the ceiling.

Above them, shadows moved, in the twitchy rhythm of a spider. It twisted toward them from where it hung. Darker indents for eyes and a mouth in what could have been a face seemed to appear and disappear, bubbling in and out all over. A low rumble vibrated through the air, and dread prickled her skin. The thing from the hotel room had found her.

The poor cage creaked as the shadow freed itself. Jun couldn't see where her chinchilla was behind the bent bars.

"Pickles!" Her yell was caught off as she was lifted in the air and thrown over Nikolai's shoulder. The set of knitting needles that she had just packed jabbed into her back with each step he took.

Where she had been crouching moments before, smoldering tendrils lashed out, piercing through the floorboards. The ceiling fractured as shadows pushed through. Her last view of her room was the ceiling collapsing. Thick black cracks followed them down the hall and into the kitchen.

Her dad was only a blur as they ran past him. He was stuck in his task of washing the dishes, completely unaware even as the walls broke apart and pieces of tiles and plaster exploded around him.

Jun screamed as she was practically thrown out the window. She skidded along grass that did not bend under her weight, but instead snagged across her skin. She barely felt it and shot up at once. Nikolai eased out the window a moment later and blocked her from trying to get back inside.

"I have to go back." Jun could barely hear herself; her ears were ringing in the sudden silence. "My dad!"

Nikolai took one look at her before grabbing her arm, forcing her into a run away from the house. "Stop, it's going to get him!" She dragged her feet and tried to pry her arm from his grip. "Let go of me! The house will fall down on him."

Nikolai didn't let go. It was like being dragged by a rhinoceros as they crossed the yard to the sidewalk.

"We could carry him out of there, please!" She must have finally gotten through to him because Nikolai abruptly stopped.

Nikolai sighed and ran his hand through short hair. "I don't see a way to get him out without breaking both of his arms. Did you see the way they were bent? The longer we spend in there is more time for the monster to have another shot at him."

Her blood ran cold.

"No." Jun shook her head, as if it would clear the words away. "I have to at least check on him. I'll be fast."

"That's what you said going in there in the first place.

And then I found you trying to break open a cage with that thing hovering over you."

"I won't go in. I just need to look."

Nikolai gritted his teeth, and Jun's mind raced. She couldn't get the thought out of her mind. Time restarting. Her house collapsing, and her dad laying in a jumbled mess. Broken, just like Cartwright and the earthquake. It would be all her fault.

"Please." She wouldn't be able to save her dad alone. She needed his help.

"Fine," Nikolai snapped abruptly. He turned, making his way back to her house, and Jun scrambled to keep up with her short legs.

He stopped, giving the window a breadth of six feet, examining it critically.

The inside of her house looked fine. It seemed dark. Perhaps more than usual. At the sink was her father, just as he had appeared before, still washing his oatmeal pot. There were no cracks in the ceiling that hadn't been there before. No monster in sight.

It was calm. "I think it's gone," Jun said, right as Nikolai picked up some rock and threw it through the window and into her kitchen. The rock skidded and thudded against the table's leg. Nothing happened. The rock just sat there, dirtying the floor that Jun swept on her weekend visits. Then the shadows converged and struck the rock, splitting it. It was black as if it had been burned.

Nikolai turned to look at her with an eyebrow raised. "The best thing we can do for him is to leave him alone."

Her father seemed all right. Frozen in his breakfast ritual, and nothing for Jun to do.

Though turned away from them, Jun remembered the look frozen on her father's face as he scrubbed away oatmeal from the same dented pot he had used since she was in third grade. His eyes were bleary from long hours at the office. He worked too hard.

It had made her cry, seeing him like that. Tired and still. So close and so out of reach, even though she was standing right next to him. She couldn't even pick up the stack of napkins off the kitchen table, as they were all wedged together like a brick. Jun had wiped her snot off on her sleeve. It was while staring at him—willing him to snap out of it, give her a hug, and tell her that everything was all right —that she heard it. The scrit scirt of tiny paws.

"What about Pickles?" Jun whispered in case the thing could hear. "What if it got him?"

Nikolai's expression was blank. "The squirrel?"

"Chinchilla," she said, affronted.

"Something tells me that thing was more interested in us than your pet. Speaking of which, do I even want to know what you were doing that was so important that you would risk your life?"

"It's not like I knew a psychotic shadow was going to be there," Jun muttered. She stepped away from the windowsill, her fingers so shaky that she had to keep them in fists. "I heard Pickles. Well, I thought it was Pickles. So I was going to get a closer look."

"What did it sound like?"

"I heard the little footsteps. You know, the kind made from a small animal scurrying around."

"What did you see when you followed the footsteps?"

"Pickles was frozen, but I thought maybe he wasn't? Like if I could get a closer look, I could get him to move?"

Nikolai scratched his chin in thought. "Maybe it was trying to lure you in."

"Yeah, but how would it even know to do that?" Unless it

could read her mind and somehow know that every time she passed a pet shop she would without fail stop to look at all the animals, it didn't seem plausible. "Is it even sentient? Have you encountered one before?"

Nikolai shrugged. "Beats me. I've only seen it after time stopped, but it does have a similar presence as magic. What I don't understand is why it would be after you, too?"

"I don't know, maybe because apparently I disrupted time and space and the entire universe?" Jun snorted. Not that any of this made sense. The only logical thing about this creepy monster was that it was after her. With her luck, that seemed about right.

She backed away in case the shadow creature was near. The subtle tension in Nikolai's jaw relaxed as she stepped away from the window.

Every few steps, Jun looked back until they rounded the corner. She hesitated on the driveway and then sat on the curb. She was tired. Physically, after walking for what felt like weeks. Mentally, she just didn't know what to do next.

Jun was not thrilled at the idea that Nikolai was most likely going to follow her. She could leave him again. It hadn't yet gotten to the point that she needed human interaction. Besides, it was better for her to be crazy rather than dead if Nikolai decided to change his mind.

"That man wasn't there before," Nikolai said as he pointed at her neighbor a few feet away from her on the sidewalk. It was Mr. Dawson, wearing a bathrobe over his pajamas, on a walk with his poodle, Barkley. Jun had known him her whole life, though she'd only say hello when they crossed paths.

"What do you mean?"

Nikolai frowned. "This entire time I was here, he was behind his dog. Now he's in front of it."

Jun shivered, thoroughly creeped out. "We've been stuck here too long and now you're seeing things."

Jun didn't know what that meant if Nikolai was right. Would time soon go back to normal? She got up and took a few hesitant steps closer. There was something wrong about his eyes. She couldn't remember what color they had been before, but she was almost positive they weren't black. She could barely tell where his pupils ended, just that there was only a sliver of blue left. The tiny veins in the whites of his eyes were the color of wine, so dark they almost looked black.

Though frozen, it felt as though those eyes were staring straight back at her.

Jun stepped back involuntarily. "Okay, I think that's our cue to leave." She found herself walking without thinking to the park around the block that had been a source of comfort to her growing up.

It was sunshiney, with willow trees bordering the playground, their leaves frozen in the gentle sway of the wind. Jun sat on an immobile swing. She braced her legs into the woodchips to push the swing into motion, but it didn't. She tried a few more times without success and then slumped against the chain with a loud sigh. "I wanna go home. Oh, wait, I just spent a week doing that and it was all for nothing. I just want things to go back to normal."

Nikolai looked unimpressed.

"But it's never going to be normal again." Jun held her pointer finger to her temples. Maybe if she pressed hard enough, she could force the answer out from wherever it was hiding in her mind.

"Now we're getting somewhere," Nikolai muttered.

"What do I have to do? Say a magic word?" Jun straightened up and cleared her throat. "Hocus-pocus time-refocus.

Abracadabra. Expelli-free-us. Bibbidi-bobbidi-let-us-go-idi."
She frowned as she tried to think of more words. "Presto
chango? Damn, I really was hoping that last one would
work. Oh, man, please don't tell me I have to draw penta-
grams on the ground."

Nikolai raised an eyebrow. "You weren't saying anything
when you stopped time in the first place. Not in class either
when you almost started another earthquake. What were
you thinking when you stopped time?"

What had she been thinking about when she stopped
time? "I don't know. I thought that you were going to
kill me."

"All right, that might be important. What did that
change when you thought that I was going to kill you?"

"I don't know. It made me nervous."

"And what happens to you when you feel nervous?"

Jun opened her bag, grabbing the knitting needles she
had just packed. "Usually when I'm feeling nervous or upset
or something, I just start knitting." A crease developed
between her eyebrows. "But when I stopped time, I didn't
have any of my yarn projects. I didn't even have my lucky
rabbit's foot." She paused when she mentioned rabbit's feet
and looked at the grassy lawn. She could no longer ignore
the scampering, little flashes of white color that flit about
the otherwise empty field.

It was obvious, now that she was staring right at it. It was
right in front of her. Hopping before her as if demanding to
know why she hadn't noticed it. Why hadn't she thought of
it when she was at her house? The scampering of little feet.
Obviously, it wasn't her chinchilla that she had been hear-
ing. It was the rabbit.

Sleek, pristine white fur. Little whiskers. It wasn't one of
those really fat, fluffy ones that Jun might look up on

Pinterest when she was having a bad day. No, this one had a wilder look about it. Its body was leaner and already poised to flit away, to move, to act. But more than any of that, it was the look in its eyes. Playful and mischievous.

Jun recognized that look. Felt it reverberate within her like a wave. Her mouth fell open in shock. Stopped time wasn't the first time that she had seen this rabbit.

She suddenly remembered going to the grocery store and being stressed out about some guy bullying her. He was trying to take the last box of snickerdoodles that Jun had rightfully gotten first. Wasn't there a rabbit on the cereal boxes that tumbled down on his head? Or one of the many times at school that there was an electrical issue, or the plaster fell down. How many times had Jun simply forgotten seeing a little rabbit scampering around outside? Or improbably sitting somewhere in the room—standing on its hind legs on the classroom globe, or from the top of the fish tank, or scampering around the walls watching her.

The rabbit wasn't new. No.

The rabbit had been with her for her entire life.

How had she somehow missed that?

Nikolai looked over at the field and frowned. "What are you looking at?"

15

Nikolai waited as Jun drifted off into thought. Finally, they seemed to be getting somewhere. At least Jun wasn't wasting their time denying that she was even capable of magic anymore. She seemed distracted, except that her mouth fell open in shock.

Her eyes flicked back and forth across the frozen field, tracking nothing.

"What are you looking at?" Nikolai frowned.

Jun shook her head and pointed. Nikolai carefully followed the direction of her gaze, but he saw nothing in particular. More empty field. Just grass and a couple of dandelions.

"You don't see it?" Her voice rang with disbelief, and Jun looked back across the grass as if to check something, long enough to seem like some stupid game. "Huh. Actually, that makes sense."

"How does that make sense?" Nikolai hid the annoyance in his voice. He had just spent what he could have only guessed was weeks tracking this girl down. He did not need her to run off on him again.

"It's like that time back at the library, when you were on the phone, saying that you had eyes on Evan, and you were wondering if he had anything to do with the earthquake."

"How did you know about that? I made sure that I was alone before taking that phone call. I would have noticed if you were there." Nikolai recalled the phone call; it was still fresh in his mind. The guilt, too. There had only been Evan and a few people sitting at the tables near him, the lady at the desk and one other student at the front.

"That's just it. I was sitting down on the other side of the bookcase. But you didn't see. Like I wasn't even there."

All of a sudden, he could see a shadow in his mind's eye that morphed into her as she sat at a table by the wall only a few feet from him.

Then he remembered that when they were in class, he would suddenly be aware of her and then dismiss her immediately. He assumed that she came in late and he didn't notice. He hadn't even noticed that he wasn't paying attention to her. Since when was someone in a knitted hat in neon bright colors not noticeable?

She delivered pizzas to his door and he hadn't noticed a thing. Hadn't connected her to the business class he spent hours analyzing. Or seen the obvious clue on her essay. He had to directly feel a magical spark before he became aware of her.

"So you're saying that part of your magic is about hiding out in the open?"

"What? No. There is a rabbit out there in the field. Just did a somersault. You don't even see it."

He followed to where she was pointing. There was a rabbit. Not a brown rabbit that was camouflaged into the grass, but a pristine white rabbit. Not frozen. It was tumbling through the grass, plain as day. "The hell is that?"

"Yeah, I've been seeing the rabbit the whole time. Actually, my whole life. But I never really noticed it before."

The rabbit that was now cheerily doing cartwheels. Casually. As if cartwheels were natural rabbit behavior.

He wanted to demand why she hadn't noticed something so obvious. But he knew better. This was clearly magic. "Okay," he said. "So there is a rabbit. What does that mean?"

"I'm not sure. But I think that every time before, when I made things happen, I think that the rabbit was always there. The rabbit had something to do with the magic. I just don't know why. I don't see the connection."

Nikolai never heard this mentioned or seen something of the like with other magicians. He couldn't be sure if this was unique to Jun. "You think if we catch it, it could help us figure out how it's connected to your magic?"

Just as he said it, the rabbit stood on its hind legs and looked right at Nikolai. The rabbit turned and bolted across the field, disappearing from sight.

"Damn, little guy doesn't like me. Should we chase after it?"

As Jun turned in his direction, the horrified look on her face gave him his only warning. Nikolai spun, reaching for the knives on either side of him. Only his undamaged hand could grip the handle. He hesitated for a second at the sight of a balding middle-aged man. That moment cost him as Mr. Dawson lunged from a foot away.

Nikolai jumped back, but not fast enough.

Mr. Dawson had him. Hands clenched around him with all the force of time. Nikolai's hand was forced open, and his knife clattered to the ground below. His arm felt as though it was going to get ripped apart under the pressure. The grip cut into him like knife blades. Tensing his muscles against the force of the grasp was useless, and he could feel his muscles give out under the strain.

Lines of black crept up his arm from Mr. Dawson's touch, like veins filled with shadows. There was a cold numbness under the spread.

A flash of purple broke his concentration as Jun, in her ridiculous hat, squared up against her neighbor.

"Stop! I don't want to have to do this." Her voice wavered as she held her arms outstretched in front of her.

Nikolai blinked. Was she really going to use magic? Had Jun been holding out on him? What sort of trick did she have up her sleeve?

The canister in her hand clicked, echoing across the silence.

Nikolai recognized the cylinder Jun held and jerked his head away in time to avoid the spray. Mace erupted out of the can in a wet hiss.

Mr. Dawson was hit full in the face and let go, scratching away at the liquid residue. Released, Nikolai fell to his knees, blinking away mace that hit him indirectly. He saw the outline of a handprint black as a burn where Dawson grabbed him.

Dawson stepped back, scrabbling at his eyes and shrieking.

She had that mace lying around that whole time? Nikolai refused to think about all the times she could have used it. Like on him, when he had first taken her. Why not use it on him?

Nikolai's arm stiffened, and the areas surrounding the blackened marks felt raw. He had to get up. He had to move. Nikolai clasped the burn mark, cradling it in his other hand. He'd been burned before, and it wasn't like this. He had never felt burned this deep, straight into the part that made him... him.

Dawson scratched at his face. It should have been torn up and reddened, but instead his features contorted and drooped like they were made of wet clay. Beneath hands that curled like talons, his face looked as if it had been melted off. Like skin stretched over the vague suggestion of a face. The hollow of his mouth stretched wide in a silent shriek.

Then he turned that empty face toward Jun.

Oh, hell no. That thing wasn't going to touch her.

Nikolai forced himself up and stepped into Dawson's path. "Hey, what do you think you're looking at?"

Dawson leapt at him, unnaturally fast.

There was nowhere for him to back into. With Jun right behind him, Nikolai couldn't launch out of the way. All he could do was raise his good arm and block him.

It wasn't enough. Dawson leapt forward. Nikolai saw that hand, blurred into claws. It was moving oddly slowly, as if time was once again disjointed, all of the laws broken here, until it grasped his face, blocking his vision.

The thing reached into his face and tugged.

Nikolai heard a delicate pop, and felt a sinking pit in his stomach that something was horribly wrong.

He heard the thing step away from him.

Nikolai couldn't see. His eyes were open, and he couldn't see.

No, there was something. Eyes stared back at him in the middle of all that emptiness. Eyes that he knew. They hung in the air at about five feet and ten inches. Dawson's approximate height. Shadows flicked around those eyes. They flickered into the shape of a person, and then they twitched and morphed into the mass of tendrils and limbs that had chased them.

He knew precisely the shape and color of those eyes. They were his own.

They blinked. Smokey tendrils curved under his eyes into a mocking smile.

Then they turned and blinked again, out of sight. Then nothing.

The world was a hazy gray.

16

J un clenched the mace can in her shaking palm. It all happened so fast. Mr. Dawson, from around the block, who swapped fishing stories with her dad, had ripped into Nikolai's arm.

Dawson somehow could move. He'd be completely still and then appear elsewhere. He seemed to walk in the corners and in the shadows, even when there weren't any around—at the edge of her awareness. Motionless, then blurred fast.

Now, Dawson had disappeared, and Nikolai was still.

Dawson did something to him. It was fast, but Jun saw him grab Nikolai's face. What if he had done something to Nikolai to make him like everyone else? What if he made Nikolai frozen as well?

What if she was left here all alone?

Jun edged over to Nikolai cautiously. Like a skittish wild animal.

"Jun?" Nikolai cocked his head back toward her.

Oh. So he didn't get frozen in time. That was good. "Are you all right?"

He didn't say anything.

"Nikolai?"

"I think I'm blind." Nikolai turned to face her.

Jun squeaked and then clapped a hand over her mouth. The skin on his face had turned coal black where he was grabbed. The darkness spread over his features in the shape of a handprint. His eyes were solid black across the cornea and pupils. That had to have hurt.

"How's my face?" Though his eyes were black, they stared right at her.

"It's marked where Dawson got you," Jun said, then bit her lip. This was her fault. Dawson was charging after *her* when Nikolai stopped it. Then she had to go and make everything worse with the mace. Was mace classified as a deadly weapon in California? Was she a criminal now?

"I'm not totally blind. I can sort of see you."

"How does that work?"

Nikolai stepped closer to her. "From far away, you look gray like everything else. But close up, you're a mix of white and black in thin lines. I can see your outline."

Nikolai placed his hand in front of his face and then lowered it. "I can't see my hand or anything else, though. Just you."

"Oh." That wasn't blindness. His injury had to do with the magic, somehow.

"Jun, we need to figure out how to get out of here before that thing comes back." He touched the shadowy skin on his face as he spoke. Was that mark still painful? Or was Nikolai worried about facing the creature again if he couldn't see?

Jun rubbed the back of her neck. "Got any bright ideas?"

"When you stopped time, you were anxious, and without your normal coping mechanism, you triggered magic. I think it's something you can access mentally, at least as a defense mechanism."

Access mentally? "You're saying I can think my way out of this?"

"Try it."

Stupid assassin, with stupid advice.

She was trapped here. There were literal monsters and the advice they were going with was to think about it.

What she needed, what she really needed, was someone who knew what was going on. She didn't need jerky McKiller ordering her to think. She needed someone who could actually give her good advice.

The annoyance burned into a bright point in her mind, and just as suddenly, it was released.

Something felt different. Jun frowned and listened intently. She felt a pulse of awareness, as if something behind her was watching her.

"You called?" a voice purred.

Jun spun and gaped.

Sprawled across the field was a creature that didn't exist. Her head was normal enough—she had full lips and curly black ringlets. Her breasts were uncovered and definitely human. The rest of her form was the body of a lion, with massive wings of long downy feathers that spread across her back. Sleek, feline muscle tensed and coiled under tawny fur. Claws that were thick and lethal scraped against the grass.

"What is that?" Nikolai asked in a tense voice as he stepped in front of Jun, placing himself in the path of the beast. "It's like you. I can see it."

"I think I asked for it to come," Jun murmured. She walked to Nikolai's side. "It's a sphinx."

"A *what*?"

"You know, a flying lion woman," Jun explained.

"You summoned a monster? Instead of getting us out of here?" His all dark eyes glared at her.

He was blaming her now? If it was up to her, she would have had a rainbow roll and the spicy salmon while she gossiped with her dad.

Jun took a deep breath. They needed information, and this creature came because Jun had been looking for advice. She waved to the... woman? Lion? She waved, hoping it wouldn't get her killed. "Hi, ma'am. Are you going to ask me riddles? I heard that a sphinx will eat someone who gets their riddles wrong."

"Is it my fault that they were stupid and I was hungry?" The sphinx smiled wide, showing off teeth that were curved into points.

"Jun," Nikolai said in an undertone. "What are you doing?"

"Getting us answers," Jun muttered. To the sphinx, she asked, "Can you tell me why we're here?"

"Why are any of us here?" The sphinx flicked her lion tail. Didn't that mean that she was getting annoyed in big cat language? Jun had to come up with better questions.

"I mean why are we *now*? Why are we trapped in this moment?"

"Shouldn't you ask that of yourself?" The sphinx extended her wicked claws, examining them like a manicure.

Jun shook her head. "I don't know the answer. That's why I'm asking you."

The sphinx scoffed. "Do you not remember what you asked for?"

Asked for this? Did the sphinx mean ask for magic? Heat flushed through Jun's body at the unfairness of it. All those years of bad luck. She'd never asked for any of this. "Magic has never given me what I asked for. My job is crap, my roommate is crap, and I can't even go on a date without the guy falling into a ditch or catching on fire somehow."

"Why do you blame the magic? Did you not question your own preference in mates?" The sphinx looked at Nikolai and raised an eyebrow. "Do you really wonder why the light tries to protect you from yourself?"

Wait, what? Jun felt dissed by the lion-lady somehow.

But that wasn't important. How was light supposed to protect her? What did that have to do with magic?

"I'm not looking for protection. I just want everything to go back to normal," Jun snapped.

The eyes of the sphinx were contracted wide, like a cat who spotted a mouse. "Which normal? The normal that makes you feel comfortable? The normal where you have no idea who you are and what you can do? The normal where the light and dark fight to claim you?"

Great. More cryptic talk about light and dark when Jun was trying to find out about magic. This wasn't helping. The sphinx was just answering her questions with more questions.

"I just don't want to be here. I want to get back to the real world." Jun's voice shook as she crossed her arms.

Beside her, Nikolai tensed as well. He gripped his knife in his hand, and his eyes tracked the twitching tail of the sphinx warily.

"Why would a place that is not here be any more real?" Her voice was dangerously playful, like a cat toying with her prey.

Jun shook her head. This was real? How could that be? Everything was frozen and there were monsters. Hell, Jun was talking to a sphinx right now.

Unless this meant that under the magic, this was still the real world. Not something going on in her head. Not some dream. Which meant that actions here would have real consequences. Either way, Jun had to get out. Had to fix it somehow. "If you know the answers, can you help me?" Jun eyed the deep gouges the sphinx carved into the earth with her claws. "Please?"

"What good are answers when you ask all the wrong questions?" The sphinx held one claw up to her forehead as if she were staving off a headache.

Why were even the monsters getting annoyed with her? This magic stuff needed to come with a manual. "What's the right question?"

"Why don't you try asking yourself what problems you have with the truth?" The voice of the sphinx was smug, like a cat that got the canary. She probably enjoyed insulting Jun. "Is there any answer that isn't already within you?"

Jun gaped at the sphinx. Problems with the truth? Did that make Jun a liar? But she wasn't a liar, besides lying to her dad sometimes. Was she?

"Anything else?" The sphinx stretched out her claws, ruffling her feathers.

Something tugged at Jun. It could have been nothing, but the worry that it wasn't wouldn't go away. "Yeah, what's up with the fortune cookies? Should I have trusted them?"

"You've read your fortune?" the sphinx hissed. Her pupils contracted into cat-like slits.

"Uhh." Was she not supposed to? It wasn't like those things came with warning labels. "Just every once in a while. I like Chinese food."

The sphinx shook her head. "How have you survived so long?"

The sphinx rolled her wings back, extending them out

to their full width. She snapped her wings against the ground once, twice, and then was airborne.

It didn't take long before she was over the clouds.

"She flew away," Jun informed Nikolai. She held her hand over her eyes, watching the sphinx disappear from view. How could a fortune cookie scare off a monster with the teeth and claws of a lion?

"What the hell were you doing?" Nikolai had put his knife away and was back to glaring at her. "Were you antagonizing that thing on purpose?"

"What are you talking about?" She'd just tried to get them answers. Following his stupid advice in the first place.

"You were complaining to a man-eating monster about your roommates and boyfriends." Nikolai shook his head like he couldn't believe she'd do that.

"Well, of course it sounds bad when you say it like that," Jun muttered.

"What was up with you? It was like you had completely forgotten that the situation was dangerous." Nikolai ran his hand through his hair, scowling at her. "Why were you being rude to a creature that could kill you?"

"No, I wasn't." Jun frowned.

"Never mind, then." Nikolai sighed. "Why did you ask about the fortune cookie? What happened?"

Jun thought back to the moment after she snapped apart the crisp wafer. "My last fortune cookie told me to run."

"Did you?"

"No." Jun shook her head. It was just a weird cookie and she had to get to work. "About forty minutes later I ran into you." Jun gestured to the frozen park around them. "You remember the rest of it."

"Do you remember any other fortunes?"

How was she supposed to remember every time she ate

a cookie? "I don't know. Something about a bag." A bag. Jun paused. The new bag hanging from her shoulder—the bag she'd been drooling over for weeks. She only bought that bag when her other one had snapped. "Oh. Shit."

"What?"

"That was the day of the earthquake," Jun whispered. Was the sphinx right?

Nikolai rubbed his eyes as if he could wipe away the blindness. "Maybe we should go get you another one."

"The sphinx was pretty clear that fortune cookies are not a good idea for me."

"Maybe not, but it's the only clue we have. I passed by a Chinese restaurant on the main road about four blocks away." Nikolai stepped cautiously back toward the sidewalk.

"Wait," Jun said. If they were really going to do this, they might as well do it right. "There's another restaurant by the Safeway I want to try."

17

Nikolai tripped and fell hard to the ground, barely catching himself. He managed to get a mouthful of grass and dirt clumps from his surprised gasp.

"Sorry, I meant your other left," Jun said.

He swiped at his mouth, brushing away moist earth and stones. This was the second time he'd tripped. Was Jun doing that on purpose? "How much further?"

"It's just across the next intersection. Are you sure you don't want to follow me?"

If Jun got taken out, he'd be trapped here. Nikolai shook his head.

It was like walking through a fog. Everything was a shapeless gray around him. It was quiet enough for Nikolai to hear the steady pulse of his heartbeat, until the adrenaline wore off and that too faded into the quiet. His breathing felt obscenely loud. How could he notice Dawson approaching over the sound of his own damn panting?

"Crack," Jun called out from behind him.

Nikolai slowed his walk, brushing his feet along the

cement until he could feel the cracked edge of the sidewalk. He gingerly stepped over it.

"The sidewalk ends in five feet. Joyful Noodle is just across the street." Jun pointed out the restaurant.

All Nikolai could see was a haze like gray smoke. That haze and Jun. If he focused, Nikolai could see the thin stripes that made up her outline. Didn't matter if she was behind him, or behind solid objects. He could manage to pinpoint her location if he focused.

"Any chance the door was left open?"

"No." Jun shook her head. "The lights are off. This place doesn't open until noon."

This was a risk. But what other choice did they have?

"I need you to grab me a rock." Nikolai felt a pebble pressed into his hands and resisted the urge to roll his blind eyes. "How am I supposed to break the door open with this?"

"There aren't exactly any boulders lying around here," Jun muttered. Fine strands of black and white flowed within the haze like ripples in water. Jun's outline paced before leaning over and jostling something low to the ground.

Nikolai approached in slow, measured paces. He reached down to help, his hand brushing against hers.

There was warmth, soft skin, and a faint pulse of energy until Jun pulled her hand away.

His mutinous heart sped up.

Nikolai grabbed the rock and retraced his steps back to the front of the store. "What's the layout of the restaurant?"

"There are three rows of booths to your left and four tables to the right." Jun pointed to the booths and tables as she spoke. "The path in front of you is about four feet wide leading to the counter. That's where the jar filled with fortune cookies is, next to the green Buddha statue."

"We have to make this quick. Just grab the cookies and go." This was a risk. But staying here and doing nothing was a greater risk. His blindness was a liability. He'd be useless as a defense against the creature now. "You ready?"

Jun shrugged. "About as ready as I can get for a cookie heist."

Nikolai slammed the rock into the door until he heard glass clatter to the floor.

He pushed his way through splintered edges of glass and felt the drop in temperature once inside.

Following the directions, he walked straight into the counter. He patted the surface, feeling around.

The figure of Jun grabbed his hand, placing it on top of the cold jar.

Nikolai braced himself and yanked the little jar, which felt as if it weighed over a hundred pounds. As he tugged it away from the counter and braced it against himself, the jar felt as though it weighed closer to five pounds. He pried off the lid easily.

"I still don't see what all the fuss is," Jun muttered as she reached for one. As her fingers hovered over the jar, the cookies appeared to Nikolai in the gray haze. One by one, they were struck through with color, some bright white and the others a solid black.

"They changed. As soon as you got close to them. They're all black or white." These colors were like those that made up Jun. They had to be the colors of magic.

"Which is this?" Jun's hand hovered over a cookie in the jar.

"That's a white one."

"Let's try it." With the snap of the cookie, a bright ripple flashed across the restaurant in a blinding ring of light.

Nikolai winced at the burn of light in the haze, as after-images obscured his view.

"It just says, 'catch the rabbit,'" Jun said, her voice indifferent. "What about this one?"

"That's one of the black ones." As Jun reached for it, the darkened patch on Nikolai's palm twitched. It was as if a foreign body jerked within him, fighting to get out.

He tightened his hand into a fist as tight as it could go. Holding in whatever it was. Worry bloomed, knotting up his stomach. Something was happening to him. They needed answers, but was this worth it?

Jun snapped open the cookie and the entire room was plunged into shadow. Darkness blocked out everything for a moment. The shadows started to dissipate back into the haze of gray, except for thickened blotches that remained.

Jun read the dark fortune. "It says, 'Go to the shadows.'"

As she read, the darkness solidified into the shadow of a person—small and crouched low. In a jerky, mechanical move, the shadow twisted its head toward them.

"Jun, get the fuck out."

"What? Why?"

"Go!"

Nikolai heard the clatter of her footsteps as he launched himself toward the shadow figure. His shoulder slammed into a table, knocking him to the side, as the figure rushed to intercept Jun. Darting forward, Nikolai grasped the dark silhouette by the ankles, grabbing hold of dry skin that felt like wrinkled leather.

With a hiss it turned, clawing deep into Nikolai's arms and cheek, ripping away bits of skin. The thing grabbed hold of the meat of Nikolai's forearm and latched on. Though the hand was small, the grip was inhuman.

Fingertips dug in, breaking skin. Nikolai couldn't see his own arm, but he could see the lines of black spreading like cracked ice in the place where his arm should be. The lines thickened into a dark web in the shape of his arm. As it spread, his fingers jerked in a spasm.

His hand twisted and turned, reaching for him. Nikolai kicked sharply at his arm, unable to feel it, unable to stop it, as it pressed down slow against his own throat. Nikolai gasped, forcing in as much air as he could hold as the familiar shape of his hand choked him.

Then pressure, closing in on his neck and all around him. Cutting off breath and thought. Every muscle tensed, straining and helpless. Nikolai clenched his jaws shut, forcing himself not to exhale out. Forced himself to hold on to the little air that he had left. His free hand grasped his throat, trying to pry off the fingers that felt welded on, immovable.

Footsteps jarred his attention from his imminent death. What the hell? He forced his neck to twist in the direction of the sound.

"No!" Nikolai said, losing air. That silhouette was Jun. What the hell was she doing?

She stepped hesitantly, but closer. "Get away from him."

Nikolai opened his mouth to warn her off. To get her out of there. All that came out was a strangled gurgle.

Jun was holding something. He couldn't see. Maybe the bear bag? What was she...

Bright light like a supernova flooded the room. The shadow let him go, snarling, as the weight on his neck loosened.

Nikolai drew in a raspy breath, easing the crushing tension.

Jun reached down and placed her hand lightly on his chest. At her touch, there was a warm flicker of energy, a rush of wind.

Then a disorienting flip, changing everything.

18

J un held on to her knees, catching her breath. "Are you going to tell me what that was all about?" She turned around to find that she was talking to no one. What? Nikolai wasn't right behind her?

He didn't get out. Crashes and bangs came from inside the Joyful Noodle.

Nikolai was a big guy. He'd be fine. But Jun crept closer to get a look at what was going on.

On his back, grimacing in a tangle of struggling limbs, Nikolai was in the grip of a wrinkled man—a man with lines of black streaming from his eyes and hands. Even from outside of the building, Jun could hear the man hissing. His jaws were spread wider than possible for a human. From within, a forked tongue flicked.

Shit.

What could she do? Should she distract the shadow-man?

The outside of the restaurant looked different. Everything was still, suspended in a moment. Immobile. But somehow different.

It was the shadows. They stretched out longer. The very air felt weighted by darkness.

How was that possible?

A prickling at the back of her neck caused Jun to slowly look up.

The sun, hanging just above the tree-line, was starting to eclipse. The burning yellow disc was slowly being eaten away as the shadows stretched closer to her.

From where it formed a humble line across the ground, the shade grew. Slinking and snaking near. Eating up the light with relentless hunger. Jun backed away from the wall of night closing in on her from all around. There was nowhere to go.

Already, the sun was a thin crescent.

The darkness thickened and writhed as if it was a living thing.

And within the gloom, something was watching her. Waiting. The longer Jun looked into the darkness, the more she was sure of it. Something was looking back at her. Calling to her.

Jun backed away into the middle of the street. As far from the shadows as she could manage. The sunlight faded.

A line of trees cast a shadow that spread toward her.

There was nowhere to go.

"Catch the rabbit," Jun whispered.

As if her words drew his presence, there he was. The white rabbit was across the street, playing in a patch of sunlight.

Jun ran for him, weaving around the patches of darkness.

"How do I? Oh," Jun said as she stood in front of the rabbit. In her hands, she still clutched one half of a fortune cookie.

"Hey there, little guy." Jun held the cookie out. The rabbit stood up to attention, sniffing delicately at the vanilla confectionary.

"That's a good rabbit. Very good rabbit. Do you want the cookie?" Jun held it out closer, letting the rabbit get a good, deep sniff.

"Go get it." Jun tossed the cookie into her bear bag and the rabbit darted after it into the bag. Jun flipped the cover over the sound of him munching.

Gotcha.

The shadows drew away as she stepped near, and Jun cleared a path back to the Joyful Noodle.

There, Nikolai was on the floor, his face contorted. The man that wasn't a man dug fingers into Nikolai's shoulder, piercing through the skin like claws. Blood was leaking out of the wound and beginning to pool on the floor.

"Get away from him!"

The thing ignored her.

As if by instinct, Jun wielded her bear bag like a weapon. She lifted the cover, revealing the rabbit inside.

The thing dropped Nikolai, snarling. Withdrawing fingers that were coated red to the knuckle. It stepped back into the shadows and disappeared within them.

Silently apologizing, Jun placed her hand on Nikolai, not touching the injured shoulder. With her other hand, Jun brushed the sleek fur of the rabbit.

With that touch, light reverberated within her until she felt it deep in her core.

Please.

The light hummed in anticipation.

This is getting out of hand. Everything just needs to go back to before this all happened. Please take me back. Let me fix this.

Light gathered, vibrating with the electric pulse of life.

Then it ricocheted outward, taking them with it.

19

6 :54 a.m.

RICHARD DAWSON WAS SKEPTICAL AT FIRST. THE IDEA OF sleeping pills seemed... excessive. Couldn't a nice cup of chamomile do the trick? He didn't want himself at the mercy of pharmaceutical aids. But he had to admit that he felt more rested. He even got Mr. Barkley out for his walk a good fifteen minutes earlier.

It was a nice, crisp morning. Richard almost forgot how the cool air agreed with him. The sky glowed in the light pink of the morning sun. It was quiet. Before the bustle of morning commutes, the rush of people and all that hectic chaos of productivity, Richard was at peace. Mourning doves cooed, and wild turkeys clucked in the distance. As Mr. Barkley walked, his tags jingled against his collar.

Had the groomers used a new shampoo? Mr. Barkley had a really lovely curl to his champagne coat. He'd have to make sure to keep the silly old dog away from puddles and questionable dirt patches. Richard had learned the hard way that Barkley would be more than happy to roll around in the smelliest bit of nastiness he could find.

Halfway around the block, the fruit trees were working overtime. The peaches were all looking rather splendid. Only a few more days now until they were ripe. If he knocked on the door of that nice old Mr. Bear and talked for five minutes about fishing, he was sure to get a peach or three handed off to him.

Well, it was good of him to check on the old man anyhow, now that his daughter was out of the house.

Yes, the peaches were quite large. If they were anything like last year, they would be just the right amount of sweet and oh so juicy and... gone? The peach Richard had been staring at wasn't there anymore. How was that possible?

He was staring right at the glorious yellow peach fuzz when the fruit suddenly disappeared. Blinked out of existence right in front of his eyes. Richard took a hard look at the trees. It wasn't just the one fruit. None of the trees had any fruit on them.

Richard stopped in his tracks. When he looked closer, he noted mounds of pits littered around the grass. Squirrels must have gotten to them and eaten everything before he got a chance at them. What a shame. *But that's not right. I just saw them. I know that I just saw them.*

He only realized he stopped walking when he heard the sporadic jangling that announced Barkley was rolling around in fertilizer, and smears of it streaked the once pristine fur. "Damn it, Barkley!"

The dog jolted up and shook himself, wagging his tail with pride. Probably proud of himself for getting away with it. Cheeky bastard.

Richard finished his jaunt around the block, leaving

Barkley in his crate. The groomers didn't even open for another hour and a half. A dog bath was not in his plans for the day, but neither was getting the aroma of fresh fertilizer all over the place. What a day, and it was barely past seven.

Maybe all he needed was to clean his face and wake himself up a little more. Then he would be able to plan what to do. Richard made his way over to the bathroom, wet his hands and rubbed them vigorously over his eyes. He looked closer at his reflection. No, there wasn't any water still over his eyes, blurring his view.

He had no face.

Richard screamed a mouthless scream and clutched at the smooth skin covering every inch of his head. All his features in the reflection seen every day for the past forty-seven years were replaced by vague indentations in a blank mass of skin.

And then it wasn't. He had a face again. Richard patted the skin, feeling the familiar curve of his eyebrows, the light stubble across his jaw, and the slight scar he got in fourth grade when he crashed his bike into a stop sign. He was all right. It was all right.

Richard forced himself to take in deep breaths. All right.

"This is ridiculous."

The extra hour of sleep wasn't worth it. "Dr. Travinsky doesn't know what he's talking about."

Richard opened his bottle of Ambien and dumped each and every pill into the toilet, flushing them down the drain.

IT WASN'T ENOUGH PROOF. JUST BECAUSE HER PHONE'S GPS location marked her at Jack's house didn't mean that they were fucking.

Should he text her? See if she responds?

No, put your damn phone away, you're at work.

Ankush put the phone in his pocket, and his fingers twitched with the need to pick it back up again.

It wasn't like there was much else to do. Three customers entered his uncle's 7-Eleven since his shift started at five in the morning. For all that Uncle Ram claimed this was a prime commuter location, customers were sparse before the summer. They were really in the middle of nowhere.

Ankush was alone with the hum of fluorescent lights, the scent of burnt coffee, and that guy in torn jeans who spent the past six minutes trying to decide between the bag of Funyuns and the Clif bar.

Was he not spending enough time with her?

Sure, recently he had more late nights studying and the extra shifts. But he was doing it all for *her.* How else was he going to take her out to Fogo de Chão? That place was not cheap.

How else was he going to provide for her?

Did she really think that she'd be able to afford weekly manicures and cocktails if he worked at a convenience store for the rest of his life?

But really? Jack?

Didn't Jack barely avoid flunking out of his Business class? What was Jack going to do for her?

Maybe he should get her that Louis Vuitton wallet she'd hinted about. It could be an anniversary gift.

Is that her reward for cheating on me?

She could have just gone on a friendly visit. Early in the morning. Right.

His fingers drummed against the counter. Nothing interesting ever happened before seven in the morning anyway.

He checked his phone. She was still at Jack's house.

He swallowed down the curses he wanted to fling at Jack. At her. How could she do this to him? He tapped out a quick message. *Thanks for being a cheating whore. We're done.*

Ankush let out a deep breath and moved his thumb over to the x button to delete it.

Glass shattered in a bang like a gunshot. The door to the frozen food slammed open and cracked, though no one had been anywhere near it.

Ankush stared at the broken glass, slack jawed, until his attention was diverted to the cash on the counter that had definitely not been there before. What the hell was this?

"Hey!" Ankush called out thirty seconds late as Mr. Funyuns-Clifbar ran out with both snacks.

Whatever. Never mind that. He had to call his uncle. They might even need to shut down the store for the day.

"Oh, shit." Ankush stared at his phone in horror. The text had sent.

Bobbie Bear skimmed through the letter from the Summit Medical Center until he found the results that he was looking for. He glanced over references to the blood work and elevated HCG levels and the CT scan results that showed one mass was getting larger. He crumpled it up and tossed it across the room into the trash can.

He had to tell her.

No. It would completely derail her studies, and Jun only had a month to go. He could hold out for that much longer.

But she deserved to know. Perhaps they could spend the last few weeks together.

Bobbie sighed and picked up his rubber gloves to finish the last of the dishes.

He couldn't screw up her degree for that. If he did, where would that leave her? What would happen to her when he was gone? Her graduation was in four weeks. They still had time.

A metallic crash and a high-pitched shriek came from within his house. Bobbie dropped the mug he was washing —the one Jun got him last Father's Day with the message "Education is important, but fishing is importanter." The handle snapped off. Bobbie held the broken pieces for a moment and tried to see if they would fit back together before he shook his head. He stalked off in the direction of the crash.

"Pickles!"

The three-tiered cage had crashed to the floor, with Jun's pet trapped and scrabbling at the bottom.

20

The rush of sound was a jumbled mess of honking cars, wind, cawing, talking. Nikolai pressed his good hand to his ear. There was so much noise.

"Can you do something to help him?" Jun said to someone.

Intense light blocked out the haze. It drew nearer. Painfully bright, filling everything. Shutting his eyes did nothing to cut the glare. Like staring into a sun plucked out of the sky. The light made contact—a soft but solid tap on his forehead from a hand that wasn't human.

With that touch, the light dimmed. As it faded, details emerged.

The world was gray. But it was no longer a haze.

"That mark on your face is gone. Can you see now?"

Nikolai nodded.

He could see. As if the world was a black and white movie. Cars, blades of grass, swaying trees. People walking into a building. All in shades of gray.

The white rabbit sat at the source of the light. Now chewing on a piece of grass.

Nikolai pressed his palm over his eyes, blocking out his vision. Just to be sure. Even with his sight restored, when Nikolai closed his eyes, he could still see the light—glaring like a miniaturized sun in the exact place where that rabbit sat.

"Jun, that's not a rabbit." The sphinx had mentioned light. Could this odd little animal be what she was talking about?

She sighed. "I know." All of her pastel tones were muted gray. Without the violent purple of her hat, she looked smaller somehow. Ephemeral and lovely. "What is it?"

That energy coiling and humming within the light. Nikolai had felt it before.

"I think the rabbit *is* magic. Not just magical. Magic itself."

The rabbit stopped eating and was standing on its hind legs, waving at him and then clapping.

Jun looked away. "What about the other one?"

The creature?

Did magic dwell in that thing of smoke and shadows? Nikolai recalled the tendrils. Like greasy, twisting lust filling the air. Heavy.

"Yeah, probably. A different form of magic." Nikolai brushed his thumb across his cheek. The scratches there felt like they had been healing for weeks, not minutes. The sharp pain in his arm was reduced to a dull throb. He'd never encountered magic used to heal.

How did this work, though? Where were they? They'd been inside of a Chinese restaurant, and now the magic had dumped them in the middle of a field.

The building looked familiar. The columns and the arched windows, the pinnacles on the roof. Those lamp lights. This was Jun's college.

But there was something off.

A girl walked by in a shapeless shift dress with a white collar. Long hair set back with a headband, but oddly bumped up.

In the street, there was a Ford Thunderbird and a Plymouth Barracuda. All car models from the late 1960s. And something told Nikolai that this wasn't a vintage car festival.

"Hey, Jun?"

"Yeah?"

"Is everything in black and white because we've gone back in time?"

"What are you talking about? I don't see anything in black and white."

Nikolai sighed. He was just colorblind, then. At least it was an improvement over being *blind* blind.

Jun held her hand up like she was stopping traffic. "Wait. What do you mean back in time?"

"Look at the cars. The outfits."

Jun turned a full 360 degrees, holding her hand to her brow to block out the nonexistent glare from the sun. She stared so obviously at a guy in a plaid sport coat that he winked back at her. "We went back in time. *Shit.*"

"You weren't trying to go back? Think. What exactly did you ask for?"

"I just asked to go back to before all this started." Jun shook her head. Eyes wide. Like she had no idea how this could have happened.

"So you did ask to go back in time."

"Not this far! I meant to go back to before time stopped."

"Magic isn't paying attention to what you meant."

"You aren't helping." Jun crossed her arms and glared at

him. How the hell did he get roped into teaching a magician?

"All right. You said you wanted to go back, but what we want to do is go forward. To move past the moment we were stuck in."

"Fine, I'll just grab the rabbit and try it again."

"Where did the rabbit go?" Nikolai looked at the empty patch of lawn where the rabbit was just sitting.

"Shit!"

Nikolai scanned the perimeter for movement as Jun chanted a litany of curses. The concrete was pale all around. A camouflage for light fur. This would have been so much easier if he wasn't colorblind.

There.

The rabbit was at the top of the staircase, its back to them. Nikolai saw a blur of white as the rabbit darted after a young couple into a building.

"That way." Nikolai pointed.

Nikolai jogged up the stairs, trying to look like he was late for a class and not like he was desperately chasing after small magic animals.

Inside was a hallway, doorways on both sides and no rabbit in sight.

"Should we split up?" Jun panted, clutching at her side.

"No. I am not getting stuck in the 1960s."

Jun opened one door and poked her head in. "Oh," she said in a loud whisper. "Sorry. Wrong class." She closed the door slowly.

Nikolai stopped himself from rolling his eyes. "Come on. We got to cover more ground."

Down the hall, and nothing. The corridor ended in a staircase with neither hide nor hair of the rabbit. Jun rounded the corner, crashing head-on with another student.

Papers spilled everywhere, and Jun toppled backward. Nikolai caught her before she fell.

He felt Jun tense as she made eye contact with the student she had collided with.

Which was odd, because that student wasn't intimidating at all. Short, like Jun. Cropped black hair with dangling circular earrings. She wore a striped pullover and jeans.

"Another Asian," the woman said. "Here, I thought I was the only one in the school."

"Sorry," Jun sputtered before darting to the floor, picking up papers and rearranging them so that they were orientated the same way. Pausing on one. "Bob? You're working with Bobbie Bear?"

"Group assignment. Why, you know him?"

Jun smiled, looking at the name. "He's really nice."

The student nodded thoughtfully as she took the papers back. "Thanks, I'll see you around."

She waved and continued down the hallway.

Jun stood frozen.

Before Nikolai could ask her what was going on, she ran down the stairs and out the doorway.

What?

Weren't they supposed to be tracking down a hairy escape artist?

Nikolai shook his head as he jogged down the stairs. Didn't take long to find her. Jun hadn't gone far. Just to a nearby bench surrounded by redwood trees.

He had been about to ask her if she wanted to be stuck in the 1960s with polio and gelatin molds, then snapped his mouth shut.

Tears trickled down Jun's face, and her shoulders shook

in silent sobs. Her doe-like eyes, pained. She was so small and hurt.

His limbs felt heavy as he swallowed. Nikolai wanted to give her a hug. But the last time he had tried to comfort her, Jun panicked.

Tentatively, he slid onto the bench next to her. "Why are you crying?"

Jun sniffed and wiped angrily at the tear marks on her face. "I killed her."

Nikolai stilled.

He closed his eyes, trying to hold back the wave of disappointment rising within. When had she lost control of her magic? He hadn't even noticed. "How did you kill her?"

"I told her Bobbie Bear was nice. Why did I have to say that?"

What? "That isn't how killing works."

"She's going to start dating him. They'll get married. Try for years to have a kid. Then in her late forties, her stupid miracle baby is going to cause severe bleeding during labor." Her chin trembled, and she pressed a fist to her lips.

How could she possibly know all this about a woman she'd just bumped into? Another Asian woman, though. Her approximate height. Nikolai stared at her blankly before it clicked. "She's your mother."

This must have been Jun's first time meeting her. What was it her mother said that triggered the crying spell? *I'll see you around.*

Oh.

"She was my mother. If she wasn't, she'd still be alive." Jun looked away as another tear trickled down her cheek.

Slowly, like he was approaching a wild animal, Nikolai reached out and brushed it away. Tracing smooth skin, taking away the smallest bit of her hurt. "You can't blame yourself. People are going to make their choices. You can't control that. They are going to feel how they feel and do what they are going to do."

Jun just shook her head.

How could he make her understand?

Nikolai glanced at the burn scars on his forearm. "When my brother died, my mom couldn't handle it. Took off on a country road and wrapped her car around a tree."

That made Jun frown at him. "Maybe it was an accident?"

"She left a note." *I love you, and I'm sorry.* Nikolai hadn't told his father.

Before it happened, his mom had gone quiet. Stopped crying. Stopped eating. Spent hours alone lying in bed with the lights off. As if Mikhail's loss had sucked all the good out of her life.

Nikolai could relate to that silent pain—he'd felt it, too. The loss broke something inside him, and he'd had to live with those jagged edges.

"Because she lost a son? But what about you?"

"What about me?"

"Why wouldn't she want to live to see her other son?"

"If you had met my brother, you'd understand." Nikolai sighed. His brother's shoes were too much for the likes of him to fill. Larger than life. Heroic. "He was always a better person than me. I was supposed to be the one killed, but he pushed me out of the path of the fire. Maybe if he hadn't, he and my mom would be alive. But blaming myself for living won't bring either of them back."

Her eyes were still sad, but Jun wasn't crying anymore. "Thanks. For listening and stuff." She sniffled, wiping her face on her forearm. "I guess we should go back to bunny tracking."

Her bag rustled. When Jun snapped it open, the rabbit popped up, front paws high in the air, like he was bursting out of a cake.

"There you are! Can you take us back to our own time? But not stuck in that moment. Just back to the normal progression?" Jun asked the rabbit. "Right. Does that make sense?"

The rabbit nodded vigorously in reply.

Nikolai gazed out into the past. It was eerie, yet familiar. Soon to be out of reach. Somewhere out there, his mother was still alive—though probably still in diapers. He sighed. Nothing he could do would change her loss in the present.

"Ready to try this again?" Jun reached for Nikolai, palm out. He took Jun's hand and let her lead him back into the future.

There was a faint pop like a bomb the size of an ant bursting and a rush of movement—the movement of decades passing by all around them. Then it stopped.

Nikolai took a steadying breath before opening his eyes.

They were still on the bench by the redwood trees. A guy walked by in artfully ripped jeans, Converse shoes and gauges. On the street was a Toyota Camry and Honda Accord.

Everything was still in black and white and shades of gray.

Damn it.

Still colorblind.

Nikolai let go of Jun's hand.

He had found the magician, and she was more powerful than most. If she lost control, the casualties would be in the hundreds of thousands.

The magician in question was currently looking around her campus. Her eyes still a bit swollen from crying.

No.

Jun had saved him twice from the creatures controlled by shadow, then she brought him back to their time. When, if she wanted to, she could have left him to die alone. She was a magician, but not his enemy.

Besides, he didn't kill innocent people. Jun, whatever her capabilities were, was innocent.

The others wouldn't see it like that.

"Jun, you have to stop going to class."

"What?" Her eyes widened.

Not even Nikolai knew if the others could be trusted. "I'm not going to do anything," he said, "but I'm not the only one hunting you."

21

Roman carefully applied a second coat of his lip balm, checking the rear-view window to make sure that it was even. You could never be too careful with skincare. He paused and fixed some hair that was out of place, frowning at the new strands of gray.

A thump from the back of the van interrupted his preening and he scowled. Roman flipped a switch and turned the *Turkey in the Straw* jingle up as loud as it would go. Roman opened the divider to the back of the truck. He'd have to take care of this himself.

Trussed up in the back of the ice cream van, their suspect was sawing his binds against the corner of the fridge unit.

That idiot David hadn't even noticed.

Roman glanced at the empty playground they were parked next to. He grabbed the window—covered in stickers of strawberry eclairs, fudgsicles and ice cream sandwiches —and slid it shut.

Roman reached down and pulled the gag out of Rick Abbot's mouth.

"Shhhh," Roman admonished him, stroking Rick's chin at knife point. "You wouldn't want me to have any misunderstandings, now would you?" Roman dug the knife deeper as Rick whimpered.

Pathetic.

"Now then, since I have your attention, what do you know about the earthquake?"

"Nothing! I told you, I don't know anything."

"I don't think I believe you." Roman grabbed his wrench, examining it in the light. Adjustable. Clean. Dinged in places, true. But still serviceable. "Let's see if this jogs your memory."

Roman cracked the wrench down like it was a whip. He loved that—the jarring impact of bone against the metal, how his hand became numb with the force of it. The smooth glide of the motion, the arc and loop of his swing. As it rose and fell, again and again.

"What? Done already?" Roman asked the hollowed-out husk of the boy's face.

Roman lifted the wrench, now covered in blood, and scrutinized it. Finding no new dents, he wiped it clean on the suspect's corpse.

"Seems like this one wasn't our elusive culprit after all," he called over his shoulder to David. "Help me with this before it gets all over the floor."

Together, they hauled the body into the freezer. David hastily shoved some of the Chipwiches out of the way.

"They're our best sellers," David explained, tossing them over the body. Two spots of red flecked his sleeve.

What a shame. David had the right temperament. Too bad he was just so sloppy.

"See, David? This is why I invest in water resistant shirts," Roman said. It was doubtful that David would be able to mend his ways. People rarely changed. He'd do for now, of course. Before he became another liability.

"Pistachio is going to be pissed that he has another body to process," Roman mused. "Would you be a dear and pick up some sodium hydroxide? Home Depot should have some. Or Walmart."

"Why doesn't Nikolai do any of the dirty work?" David muttered.

"Nikolai is going by the rule book, and if he's anything like his brother, he's not stupid."

David made a noise of disgust in the back of his throat. Then nudged the freezer with his foot. "Is this going to be a problem?"

"Hmm. People disappear all the time. Especially when there's a magician around. Don't worry, the more murders the magician has under his belt, the bigger the payout when we get him."

"Who's next on the list?" David asked.

Roman took out his cellphone and opened his Photos, then scrolled through pictures of Nikolai's notes to a list of class names. Really, if Nikolai didn't want the competition, he should have purchased a better lock.

"Bailey Allen."

22

The gyro wasn't bad, actually. Just a pinch too salty, and the sauce would benefit from a touch of acid. But the flavors were there. It was fresh. Jun didn't know why she had never eaten here before. Maybe she hadn't noticed it. It wasn't because her college's food court was large. That wasn't it. Right next door was Happy Dragon, lit up in flashing neon, with that siren call of fried wontons. If she had just gotten Kabob King on her lunch break weeks ago, she wouldn't have had to deal with all this fortune and earthquake drama.

A hulking figure blocked out the LED light. Jun swallowed. "What?"

Nikolai pulled out the chair across from her and sat down. "It's been two weeks. Why are you still working here?"

"For the money, mostly. And the employee food discount." Jun took another bite. She wasn't going to let an over-muscled worrywart get in the way of her well-deserved lunch break. She had earned this.

"You are way too accessible here. Did you know that you're registered in the work study program? Do you know how long it takes to look you up in the system?"

Jun took another bite. If Nikolai wanted her to pay more attention, he should have come when she was eating a crappier lunch.

"Three minutes. It took me three minutes to find your name as an employee here."

"I've been fine. None of your friends has even ordered anything, and they wouldn't recognize me even if they did."

"Because I told them that pizza is ruining my diet. I had to follow through with that, too. You don't want to know how much kale I've eaten in the last week."

"Oh, heavens! You had to eat kale? I'm so sorry."

Nikolai gave her a dirty look, and Jun held back the impulse to stick her tongue out at him. She was a mature adult, after all.

"Why don't you have a new phone?"

"Pickles needed emergency surgery. It ate up a good chunk of my savings." Jun dropped the rest of her gyro onto her plate. The reminder killed her appetite. "Little guy lost his foot."

Nikolai lowered his voice. "Is that from the time thing?"

Jun nodded. It could have been worse. He could have died. Chinchillas were fragile. They were lucky that the shock didn't give her little buddy a heart attack.

Nikolai reached into his pocket and pulled out his cellphone, placing it in the middle of the table. "Here."

"Yes, you have a very nice phone." Jun raised an eyebrow at him.

"It's for you."

"What?" Jun pushed the phone back across the table. "You can't just buy me a phone."

"It was my fault that your old phone was destroyed. Consider this a replacement."

"But this is a new model. It's, like, over a thousand dollars."

"It's supposed to be waterproof and shatter resistant. I'll send you a text if the others get too close."

The reminder of Nikolai's team squashed Jun's protests. And the phone logo was shiny—Jun could see her face in it. "I thought they didn't know anything about me?"

"Things are too quiet. They're up to something." Nikolai frowned. "Are you still going to go to class?"

"I'm graduating in less than two weeks."

"You're putting yourself in danger."

"You worry too much."

Nikolai shook his head at her.

Fine. Let him shake his head. But she was fine. Lightness eased through her, settling in her bones. Things were different now—magic would protect her.

"Well, I gotta get back to work." She pocketed her new phone, resisting the temptation to check out the new high resolution in front of him.

"You gonna finish that?" Nikolai pointed to the sad, forgotten gyro on her tray.

"Have at it, kale-boy," Jun said, jamming her Feelin' Saucy cap back on and walking across the campus dining hall to get to work.

Jun nodded to Alexa at the register as she grabbed the keys to the Crust.

"That the guy who was giving you trouble?" Alexa nodded toward the table Jun just left.

"Yeah, but it's fine. We worked it out."

Alexa smirked. "You didn't tell me that he's hot."

Jun shrugged.

Nikolai was currently inhaling the rest of Jun's lunch. Not savoring it or anything. That gyro deserved better.

"His six packs probably have six packs. I can tell."

"Um, yeah. I think he works out." Now that he wasn't a threat, Jun could admit it—there was something compelling about all that raw strength.

"You say it like you're not tapping that."

"I'm not." How could she even describe her relationship with Nikolai? They weren't enemies or acquaintances. He kept popping up in unexpected places, nagging her to be safe. "We're just friends."

"You could try flirting with him."

"I don't think he sees me like that."

Alexa muttered something that sounded like "oblivious" and "waste."

Whatever. Alexa could think what she wanted. Nikolai was following her around to make sure she didn't cause a bit of mass destruction.

Minutes later, Jun sidled into the Crust, inhaling the familiar smell of melted cheese and garlic. She turned the keys and switched on the radio. Jun took off her hat to adjust it and out hopped the white rabbit. He settled himself on the console and waved to Jun.

"Why, hello there." Jun smiled back, then gestured at the car radio apologetically. "Sorry about the commercials."

The rabbit thumped his hind leg, and the radio announced, "And now back to music, with Ellie Goulding's 'Lights.'"

"Oh, sweet, I love this song!"

Jun delivered the pizzas, her rabbit friend riding on her shoulder and occasionally on top of the pizza boxes.

None of her customers noticed him. Not even Mr. Shattuck Ave., who dissolved into a fit of sneezes a minute into opening the door. He paid for the pizza and turned back inside awkwardly. Overall, it was a very excellent day.

Class also went well, as soon as she managed to ignore the glares that Nikolai threw her way. Well. If looks could kill, she'd be in trouble. But they couldn't. Jun would be fine.

He texted her three times.

If I see anyone from my team, I'm going to text you to run.

You need to be more aware of your surroundings.

You should try sitting closer to the exit.

All this stress couldn't be good for his blood pressure. Probably a good thing that he was adding kale to his diet.

But the class ended without incident, like it had every other day for years.

As the class let out, Jun slipped into the bathroom—ink smudges and knitting did not mix. Her latest project was silk wool and she was not going to risk it.

She reached for the faucet and gasped.

Tendrils of darkness twisted out of the drain, reaching for her.

Jun backed away, heading slowly to the exit.

The darkness drifted into the shape of a hand that stretched out to her. The index finger curved, beckoning. More black tendrils flooded out from the drain, obscuring the bathroom like smoke.

Jun pressed herself against the door as the shade loomed closer.

She knew exactly what it wanted.

Go to the shadows.

Jun rushed out of the bathroom, only slowing when she was sure that thing wasn't following. Not that running would help.

She hadn't left the creature behind in that space where time stood still.

This time her fortune wouldn't be ignored.

23

Nikolai sighed as he put the phone to his ear. She wasn't going to like this.

She answered on the first ring.

"Jun, your boyfriend is in the hospital."

"That sucks for him."

Nikolai paused and raised an eyebrow. She was practically hysterical when trying to save her rodent. Nikolai was expecting tears or shock or something.

"I don't have a boyfriend," Jun said in a bored voice.

"That guy who sits in front of you in class?"

"Bailey's not my boyfriend," Jun said in that same disinterested voice. Then she swallowed. In quick, worried tones she asked, "Wait. What do you mean he's in the hospital?"

"It's in the campus newsletter, since his dad's a notable alum."

Nikolai heard clicking in the background. She was probably searching it up. Good. He didn't want to explain that Bailey had three broken ribs that ended up puncturing his lung.

Jun gasped. "Oh, my God! It says he was mugged? That's really messed up! Who would do something like that?"

"My roommates."

"What?" Jun sounded startled.

"I found a UC Business ring left on the counter. Solid gold." The ring was distinctive. Nikolai had noted the style of it when Bailey walked into the back aisle to flirt with Jun.

"But why Bailey? He's totally innocent. The guy is about as suspicious as sliced wheat bread."

"That's what I need to find out. I'll call as soon as I get more information. Any chance that you'll take my advice and lay low?"

"Not with finals in a week and a half."

Why did she have to be so fucking stubborn? Nikolai tried not to think about Evan. Clumsy. As magic as mud. How his face was beaten bloody and his teeth knocked out.

Or Bailey, unconscious back in his hospital room.

"You're putting yourself in danger," Nikolai reminded her.

"I'll be fine. I'll finish up and it'll be like I was never even here."

Nikolai swallowed down all the arguments that had already failed.

Something crashed in the background. "Shit," Jun said. "Got to go."

She hung up.

Nikolai shook his head.

Something was off about Jun's reaction to danger, and this wasn't the first time he'd seen it. She had no caution with a man-eating sphinx. Hell, she'd reacted the same way to him. Oddly indifferent at times, like when he'd kidnapped her. Her reaction didn't seem like something she had control over. In fact, she didn't even seem aware that anything was wrong.

On his way out of the Emergency Room parking lot, he walked around an ambulance. The paramedics inside were eating takeout with the windows open. It smelled amazing.

Nikolai probably could have snuck away more and picked up a burger or whatever. But he always seemed to have more important things to do.

He balled up the custodial uniform and tossed it in the dumpster, after checking to see that he was out of range of the security cameras.

His team wasn't operating according to standard protocol. Nikolai already knew that. And many teams viewed the rules as suggestions rather than guidelines. But there was something off.

Roman had eased up pressure. Stopped texting for updates. Had gone quiet.

Nikolai didn't like it.

Back at Durant Ave, Nikolai peered into the common area, listening. No light on in any of the rooms. He knew from experience that Roman and Pistachio snored. At any rate, it was midday. The others were out.

Alone, then.

What were they up to?

Nikolai grabbed a banana from the counter, next to Bailey's ring.

Why leave that out in the open? Are they testing me? Nikolai wondered as he scarfed down the banana.

Standing on the foot pedal, Nikolai peered into the trash. Partially obscured by grease stained napkins, takeout containers, and apple cores was a receipt. Gingerly, he fished it out, replacing it with the peel.

· · ·

SAFEWAY FUEL STATION
   1140 Shattuck Ave
   Berkeley, CA 94709
   Date/Time 05/02/12 10:51:27
   *** FUEL ONLY RECEIPT ***
   Nozzle No: 4
   Product: Diesel
   Gallons 10
   Price/Gal $3.833
   Fuel Sale $38.33
   Thank you!
   Have a nice day!!

THEY DIDN'T MENTION ANYTHING ABOUT A CAR. FUCKERS made him take an Uber if he needed to get anywhere. But this was a receipt for Diesel. What did they need that for?

Nikolai sighed. He needed to know. With gloves and a tension wrench, Nikolai unlocked Pistachio's door and peered inside the room. It was spartan and organized. An open briefcase filled with syringes on a folding table. Next to it, a three-ring binder. A full closet with everything from button down shirts to full suits. The top shelf had a dozen bottles of what looked like hair product.

Nikolai checked the pocket of one outfit that Pistachio might have been wearing last week. It didn't even have lint. The bottles within the syringe were unmarked. Drug problem? Hypnotics? Neither told him anything.

Nikolai flipped the binder open with one finger. In no particular order, he found receipts, including the rent on the apartment. An excel spreadsheet with lists of numbers that were unmarked. Useless.

Auto insurance policy for $1,500, taken out two weeks

ago. Nikolai scanned over the document until he found a license plate.

Bingo.

He snapped a picture and flipped the binder closed.

Google provided a list of free parking spaces in the area. One thing Nikolai could count on was that his roommates were cheap. They weren't likely to pay the four hundred-dollar semester permit, or even the daily ten-dollar parking fee. At any rate, the cost wasn't anywhere on Pistachio's neat excel spreadsheet. Nikolai jogged to the parking lot closest to the campus and inspected each license plate with no luck. He found nothing in the next two areas, either.

Four hours and halfway down his googled list of free parking later, he found the truck. In all honesty, if he wasn't so hungry, Nikolai might have overlooked it. What the fuck were they doing with an ice cream truck?

He hadn't done a car lock in a long time. The pick motion was different. It required more pressure, while his index finger held the wrench flat. Out of practice, it took nearly fifteen seconds before he heard the lock click.

He had never been inside an ice cream truck before, but nothing struck him as out of place. All the surfaces were chrome and clean. The front seat was spotless, though there was a wrench on it. They might have needed that for automotive repair.

Nikolai flipped the freezer open.

He sighed when he saw the body surrounded by Chip-wiches, ice cream sandwiches and push-up pops. The face was beaten past the point of recognition. Lividity already set in the pale skin.

Going through the dead man's pockets, Nikolai was able to pull out one of those clip-on wallets. It didn't have much.

No credit cards, just thirteen dollars in cash. But it did still hold the student ID.

Rick Abbot.

A student in Jun's class.

Why? Nikolai returned the money clip as he snagged one of the ice cream sandwiches, pulling open the plastic and popping it into his mouth.

Did they even have a plan? One dead and two injured kids from the same class. It was almost too much activity. Even with intervention from Order headquarters, the police might get involved. Unless they were gambling on finding the magician fast enough to add this body to the magician's kill count.

One dead. Two injured?

A sinking feeling pooled in the pit of his stomach as he stared at the corpse. What was it that Pistachio told him? That Evan was drugged and packed off to Reno?

Nikolai took out his phone and looked up Rehab facilities in Reno. A quick search showed there were over twenty. This was going to take a while.

Two hours and three ice cream sandwiches later, there was a jangle of keys outside of the truck.

Pistachio didn't notice Nikolai in the truck at first, as he was wrestling with a garbage bag that looked to be containing something misshapen and heavy. He dropped the bag, which landed with a hard squelch when he noticed Nikolai leaning against the freezer with a half-eaten Chip-wich in hand.

"Who was that?" Nikolai pointed to the bag.

"Guy named Tom."

Another from Jun's class?

Tom Bates.

Short guy with glasses and wiry hair. Ranked twentieth

in the cohort, with an extensive list of extracurricular club affiliations. Most of them related to online gaming and cosplay.

"So you guys found the magician, then?"

"Yeah," Pistachio said too quickly.

Lies. The magician was just about to finish her shift delivering pizza.

"Rick, here. He was a magician too, then?" Nikolai tapped the top of the freezer.

"That's collateral damage." Pistachio brought the bag all the way into the van and shut the door.

"Like Evan?"

"Evan's in a rehab facility."

"In Reno? Funny. I just got through with calling. Did you know that there are twenty-three rehab facilities in Reno? And here's the fun thing. None of them have any records of an Evan." Nikolai tossed the rest of the Chipwich in his mouth, chewing thoughtfully, as Pistachio went very still. "Did you even try any of that drug rehab stuff, or was it all a lie?"

"Can't have loose ends. Too risky."

Nikolai nodded. It made sense. At least it explained why neither Roman nor Pistachio were reported in all their years in the hunting business. He slipped the ice cream wrapper into his pocket. Didn't want to leave any evidence that he was here. He unsheathed his blade, still hidden within his sleeve.

Pistachio charged, syringe out and aimed for the chest.

Nikolai dodged and slashed a line under Pistachio's chin like a second smile, snipping his carotid artery.

Pistachio gasped for a moment and clutched his throat before his eyes slipped back behind his head. He fell to the ground.

Once he went still, Nikolai wiped the blade off on Pistachio's fine cotton shirt. He had a hunch that they'd turn on him. Had been expecting it from the moment he'd discovered the contents of their freezer. It was nice of Pistachio to confirm it.

Nikolai picked up the garbage bag, jostling it to shift the contents around. It certainly felt like a body.

But Tom Bates? Bailey Allen. Rick Abbot? What was the connection? Nikolai mentally turned the names around in his mind.

Oh.

Those damn bastards. There was no connection. It was just alphabetical.

Rick Abbot.

Bailey Allen.

Tom Bates.

Jun Bear.

Fuck.

If those fuckers really were just knocking students off in alphabetical order, Jun was next.

Nikolai stepped over Pistachio and out of the truck, grabbing his phone as he went.

Jun picked up on the second ring.

Nikolai ran his fingers through his hair. Wondering how he hadn't managed to see through their bullshit earlier. Why the hell had it taken him so long?

"They're after you. Now's the time to run."

24

J un huddled under the soft Merino wool of her blanket, flashlight pointed at her chin. So far this seemed to be working, as long as the batteries didn't run out. She'd just changed them, what, an hour ago?

"What the fuck is up with the lights? Are you afraid of the dark or something?" Suzie snapped.

Up on the ceiling the creature waited, just out of reach of the light. Spider-like eyes bubbled in and out of focus on the shadows of its face.

"Something like that." Jun looked away.

The more Jun looked into the darkness, the more the darkness looked back at her. It was getting harder to hold back.

"I can't sleep like this. Stop being ridiculous." Suzie crossed the dorm, reaching for the night-light emitting a cheery yellow glow around the room.

"Leave it," Jun said.

Suzie scowled, though her finger faltered for a moment. "Don't tell me what to do."

"No! Wait!" Jun was too late. Suzie pulled the night light out of the wall.

With the loss of the light, the room was plunged into a darkness deeper than what should have been possible. Jun clenched her flashlight tight.

"Shit! Shit! Shit!" Jun scrambled back into the walls, keeping the light trained on her face as she reached out for the light switch.

She fumbled around before flicking it on.

For a moment, darkness remained. Stubborn and defiant. Then, with an audible sigh, the darkness retreated. First from the corners, then drifting away from the middle of the room. The shadows clung to a form—Suzie's form, hugging her body. The darkness seemed to melt off of her, sliding back into cracks, under beds and behind all things, where it belonged.

Suzie stood still. Too still.

The shadows were still sliding down her body, like black paint dripping.

"Suzie?" Jun asked. Shit. Shit. Shit. *Please don't have something like what happened to Dawson happen to her, too.*

Suzie turned. Her eyes were a solid black, across cornea and pupil both.

Jun's cell phone rang. "Bad Boys," the *Cops* theme song, cut through the air.

"Nikolai?" Jun answered.

"They're after you. Now's the time to run," Nikolai said.

Suzie took a step toward Jun. The movement was jerky, uncontrolled. Like she was a zombie.

"This is a really bad time. Could you, like, hold them off?" Jun backed away from Suzie, holding her flashlight out like it was a weapon.

"Are you serious? Jun, they want to kill you."

"Oh, no. I totally got that. Small problem. They aren't the only ones that want to kill me right now." The phone rattled as her hands trembled.

"What's happening?"

"That thing is after me. The creature thing. It just went into my roommate." Jun grabbed her bear bag without breaking eye contact from Suzie. Maybe if she moved slow, she could get away without Suzie noticing?

"What!"

"It's been following me around for the past few days. I didn't mention it before because I was hoping that it would go away." Jun was against the door to her dorm room, her hand behind her back, fumbling to unlock it.

Jun opened the door, and Suzie snapped her head toward the direction of the sound. With an inhuman shriek, she charged in fast, twitchy motions. Jun bolted out the door and slammed it shut.

Behind her, the door rattled at the hinges as Suzie shrieked and pounded at it.

"Where are you? We gotta get you out of here."

"No. I can't just leave." Jun braced against the door, pushing back against the body slams.

"Do you have no survival instincts whatsoever? Why not?"

"My dad." She couldn't leave without him.

"I'll try to hold them off. Get your dad and run."

"Okay." Jun hung up.

Suzie slammed into the door so hard that Jun's head jolted forward and smacked back against it. Rummaging through her bag, Jun grabbed her thickest copper knitting needle and wedged it under the door.

She dashed down the hallway, and she didn't stop to see if Suzie followed.

Out of the dorms, to the curb, Jun didn't stop until she was right under the glare of a lamppost.

"Come on, come on." Jun clicked on the Uber app, waiting for it to load up. If only her car wasn't still impounded after she'd reported it stolen.

Around her in the dim light, the shadows stirred. Jun leaned into the metal of the lamppost and clutched at her flashlight as the darkness pressed closer in interest.

Jun punched in her dad's address and watched the little car icons move around on the map. She could feel the weight of the eyes of the creature on her back. Jun would not look up. She would not.

She jumped into the back of the Uber when it finally came and flicked the light on inside of the car.

"Are you okay?" The driver frowned at her.

"Yes." In her peripheral vision, Jun could see eyes emerge in the night air, crowding against the windows of the car. The muscles in her legs tightened as Jun gripped her flashlight until her knuckles turned white. "I'm just having a really bad day."

On the road, Jun fiddled with her phone as she plotted out a reason that sounded plausible for the two of them to leave town. In short, there wasn't a good reason. They were halfway to her house. She had to say something. Nothing to say but the truth. She could try telling him the truth.

Jun went to the lone number in her phone's favorites and pressed call.

"Hello, Jun," the voice on the other line replied. It was not her father.

She clasped a hand over her mouth, holding in her gasp, as her heart began racing.

"Who is this?" Jun asked when she trusted herself to speak. But she didn't need to ask. She recognized the modulated voice who shouted Nikolai's name in his apartment. Her heart sank.

"If you want to see your father again..."

"Got it," Jun cut him off. "I'm on my way." Jun promptly hung up on him.

She leaned back against the leather seat, clenching her eyes shut. Forcing herself not to cry. No. She had to deal with this.

Jun tapped out a quick text message to Nikolai. *They have my dad.*

Out of the Uber, Jun walked the path to her childhood home. Shadows followed close on her heels. Acting on impulse, she turned off the flashlight and tossed it on the lawn. She had bigger things to worry about.

The front door was ajar. Jun tightened her first before pushing it open.

"Well, that was quick," said a red-haired man with hard eyes and an oily smile. He stood at her kitchen table behind Jun's father, hands wrapped around Bobbie Bear's throat.

Her dad was trying to shake his head at her. He mouthed, "No" and "Get out."

Jun's eyes flicked to the upper corner of the hallway where the creature swelled, eyes narrowed in anticipation. Hovering over all of them like a fog.

"It's me you want." Jun swallowed. "Please, he had nothing to do with this."

The shadows slithered down, reaching toward Jun.

"Where are my manners? Allow me to introduce myself. My name is Roman Walker." Roman pressed harder on her father's throat. Veins bulged on her dad's forehead as his face turned red.

"No! Stop!"

"I've been tasked with apprehending the criminal

responsible for the recent earthquakes, and all the evidence points to you."

"Please, stop! You're hurting him." Jun stepped closer, stopping when Roman tightened his grip in reply.

"So you won't admit it?"

"Yes! I'll admit it. Please, just let him go!" Jun saw spots. Her head felt blurry.

She heard his neck crack. It was as if she was outside of herself. Her father stopped struggling and went limp.

"What? Finished so soon?" Roman let go, and her father fell to the ground.

Jun stared. Oddly, her mind flicked to when she was seven and fell off a bicycle, and her father kissed her scraped knee and told her it was all right.

Please get up. It's all right. He didn't move.

Her father was dead.

She didn't feel panicked anymore.

Jun turned and faced Roman.

She didn't feel anything anymore.

Jun looked to the shadows. But there was no monster there. In its place was a little black rabbit that stared up at Jun with inquisitive eyes. Like it had always been. For her entire life, the darkness had always been there. It had always been waiting for her.

"Go to the shadows," Jun whispered as she took a step back into the darkened hallway. She reached back and brushed the soft downy fur of the black rabbit.

Electricity flicked up her hands, flickering into the numbness. Filling up all the raw and empty spaces in her heart where her father used to be. An electric pulse rose up within her, and the feeling was bliss.

Roman nudged her father with the toe of his boot.

"Guess I was a little too hasty there." He shook his head. "What, are you finished, too? Scared little girl?"

Roman didn't matter anymore.

Jun cocked her head at this strange, squawking creature that took away the one thing in her life that mattered.

He stepped closer to her, knife out and aimed at her stomach.

Jun pressed her palms to the ground.

The earth pulsed, shuddering beneath her as if it were liquid, as all of her rage leaked out of her fingertips. The floorboards cracked and splintered open as earth burst through.

There was a glint of steel as Roman threw a knife blade. A clod of earth rose and blocked it.

Rock and soil twisted around Roman Walker, pressing into him from all around. His face turned bright red. Jun listened to the snap of bones and the pop of eyeballs as they burst like ripe berries. His screams cut off under the pressure. He fell limp and the earth rose over him like a tide, dragging him beneath.

It wasn't enough.

Jun crossed the hall and placed her hands on her dad's still and wrinkled face.

"Wake up."

He wouldn't move. He didn't open his eyes with a smile. The hands made for cooking waffles and reeling in trout lay still.

Jun pressed her hand over his chest and released a surge of electricity through him.

"Wake up." Her hands were shaking. Electricity flickered from her fingertips. "Please." Spots flickered in and out of her vision, and her head spun. But she could see the black rabbit in the shadows. The rabbit met her gaze and shook its head.

Jun leaned over her dad and kissed his forehead, same as he had done for her every night before bed when she was little. She brushed her fingers along his eyelids, gently closing them. Her father always worked so hard. He could rest now.

It wasn't enough.

Once again, Jun lowered her palms to the floor as she opened her mouth and screamed. She screamed her throat raw. Felt the pulse of her heart as a drum in her ears. With each beat, she poured her loss and the broken edges where her father was ripped away. She felt it when the electricity struck deep, meeting the earthquake fault line.

25

Durant Ave was quiet. Nikolai opened David's room to find him sitting in front of a computer monitor displaying a chinchilla in a knitted top hat. They were already searching up Jun. But what did they know?

"Why are you looking at pictures of a squirrel?" Nikolai asked, playing dumb.

"Research." David kept scrolling through the blog and all the various costumes Jun made for her pet.

"Hasn't been much going on here. If this is the kind of research you've been doing, I can see why."

"You'd be surprised." David smirked in a self-satisfied way.

"Try me."

"Sorry, no can do. Roman's orders."

Could this guy be any less obvious? But Nikolai could play along.

"I thought we were a team, yeah? Aren't we all looking for the magician?"

"Yes. But some of us like methods that are more effective than others."

"Effective how? You've found him, then? You're on his trail?"

"Or her," David said, scrolling through comments on Jun's blog.

Nikolai's hand balled up into a fist, and he forced himself to loosen it. He was too late. Jun was already a target. "You don't need my help?"

"That's right. We got a system. And when Roman, Pistachio and I finish off the magician, we'll all split the reward."

David was completely suckered into this half-baked serial killing scheme. Was that all it took? Dangle a bit of money in his face, like a mercenary for hire?

Nikolai had heard enough. David was more than happy to implicate himself. But how committed was he to the cause?

"This system you have is legitimate, right? You guys aren't just going around in an ice cream truck murdering college kids in alphabetical order?"

David got up from the computer and turned, hands clenched at his sides.

Nikolai was hoping to see some remorse, or at least some guilt at being found out.

David showed none, instead cracking his knuckles and shaking his head at Nikolai. "What's your problem? You have, like, the highest kill rate in all of North America. Is that not enough for you? You've got to take this one away from everybody else, too?"

"I've never resorted to killing innocents." This wasn't a competition. It was supposed to be about taking out the monsters parading about in human form. Keeping people safe.

"Yes. You are so good at finding magicians and finishing

the job. And getting all the payout. You know that's why no one wants to work with you."

"That's why you think Roman and Pistachio are hiding what they're doing?" If Nikolai wasn't so busy watching David, waiting for him to move, he would have face palmed. "If their methods got reported to the Order, they'd get black-listed. Do you know what would happen to them without Order protection?"

David scoffed. "It's all for the greater good. We gotta take down the magicians somehow. Those losers we killed would probably end up dead anyway in the next earthquake if we don't do anything to stop it."

Nikolai shook his head. David didn't get it. He'd try to connect the dots for him in simple terms. "You never stopped and wondered how they managed to get away with this for so long? Pistachio and Roman have been in the business together for years. Just the two of them. You didn't think it was strange that they had to take on two newcomers to their team? Would you be so willing to help them kill people if you thought maybe you might be next on their list?"

"It's a dangerous profession." David brushed away his concern. "People get spooked and quit. Or get injured. You're just trying to make this mean something since you don't fit in here with the rest of us."

"If they're so willing to throw me out, aren't you worried that they'll do the same to you?"

"No," David scoffed. "Not everyone can get with the program. You obviously can't."

"You don't have to get mixed in with their bullshit." *Last chance.* "Just walk away."

David brought his fists up, elbows in, and swung.

Nikolai tucked in his chin and rolled with the punch.

The blow grazed his temple. Nikolai feigned a weak hit, and David came in closer.

The next blow caught Nikolai square in the stomach, winding him, and a meaty arm wrapped around Nikolai's neck. Stars burst in bright flashes. Stepping back and locking his leg behind David's, Nikolai turned and threw him to the ground.

Nikolai stopped him from getting back up with a blade between the fourth and fifth rib, just to the left of the sternum. Straight to the heart.

David blinked in surprise at the handle jutting out before muttering, "Asshole." His eyes widened when he realized where he was hit. Or maybe his reaction came from the catastrophic drop in blood pressure from all the immediate internal bleeding.

Nikolai waited until David fell limp before he eased off, pulling out the knife. He wiped the blade clean on David's hoodie.

He'd be dead in four minutes. There was no coming back from a wound to the heart.

The rest of Durant Ave was empty, with no sign of Roman.

With a sinking feeling, Nikolai reached for his phone, and one text notification lit up on the screen.

They have my dad.

A weight dropped in the pit of his stomach. Nikolai took a steadying breath and swallowed down the lump in the back of his throat.

Roman was going after the one person Jun cared about —a frail and defenseless old man. While Jun controlled some of the most powerful magic Nikolai had ever seen. What was worse, Roman was drawing her back home. Back to a densely packed suburb surrounded by hundreds of thousands of innocent people.

Nikolai was out the door, running. Jun's house was in Northern Oakland, a little over two miles away. He could make that in fifteen minutes. Thirteen if he got lucky.

The world blurred by as Nikolai sprinted. Ignoring the warning blinks of the "Do Not Cross" sign. Nearly ramming into two people. He had to move. He didn't want to think about what would happen if he was too late. He crossed about a dozen city blocks and made it most of the way.

The earth shuddered beneath his feet and rocked like waves. His momentum had him crash to his knees and scrape his palms against the pavement.

When he closed his eyes, his second sight emerged— still functioning long after his encounter with Dawson. He could see streaks of black shadow cracking and splintering beneath the shivering earth.

Up and down the street, car alarms were going off and dogs were barking. The asphalt split open, revealing a pit of earth like a gaping maw, ready to devour anyone falling within.

Nikolai braced himself. Shingles toppled from rooftops and glass shattered. He pulled himself up and pressed forward on the violently trembling ground. He had to keep going. Just three blocks away.

Beneath his feet, the earth rumbled as the sidewalk shifted back and forth. Powerlines swayed and snapped, falling to the ground in showers of sparks. Concrete rubble smashed down, creating dust clouds. Screams echoed out from inside houses.

He kept moving, though it felt as though someone had grabbed him and was shaking him without stopping. Above him, trees rattled, and branches and palm fronds fell.

Nikolai ran. He edged away from the corner where two cars collided and avoided a building with cracks running up the side.

Heaving earth knocked him off his balance, forcing him to his knees. He clenched his fist and got back to his feet, forcing himself to focus on his path that swayed and rocked in front of him. He had to stop this.

Nikolai tried to speed up when he saw Jun's house, but the shaking intensified the closer he got. Step by step, Nikolai pushed forward.

He got to the front door and shoved it open.

There in the kitchen was Jun, with her eyes all constricted. The pupils were sharp points, and a haze of shadows surrounded her.

She looked like any other magician that he had ever taken down.

His job was to protect people who had no defense against the monsters who could rip them apart. Monsters who caused earthquakes. Nikolai touched his index finger to his blade as his stomach tensed, and his breath caught in his chest. His feet felt a weight that had nothing to do with the earthquake.

This was Jun. With her stupid hat and her sarcasm. Jun, who just wanted to knit scarves and eat sushi.

Yes, it was Jun. And she was killing people.

Nikolai stepped into the shadows surrounding her, knife in hand. The shadows parted for him.

Her palms were to the floor, pumping darkness deeper than Nikolai could see. Though strange with tight pupils, it was still Jun. Tear tracks ran down her cheeks. Nikolai pulled Jun to her feet, and the dark did nothing to stop him.

Where her skin touched his, energy pulsed between them, and warmth slid up his arms.

She was such a light and fragile little thing. So easily broken. Sever the spinal cord properly and she would never even feel any pain.

He grimaced, forcing himself to look into her lost and constricted eyes. Decision made.

Nikolai held Jun's face in his hand and brushed the tear stains away. He leaned in and kissed her—brushing against soft lips and sweetness. The warmth of her touch spread through him, as his heart pounded, and his fingers laced into her hair. Every inch of him burned with the need to press closer, hold her tighter, taste her deeper.

Jun leaned into him, grabbing his waist, kissing him back. Then she blinked and pulled away. Eyes wide. Wide and normal again.

She took a deep gasping breath.

The shuddering of the ground quivered to a halt. The rattling ceased. One lone plate toppled and crashed to the floor. The earth stood still.

"Nikolai?" Jun whispered.

Nikolai nodded, as all the tension released from his limbs and unwound the knot in his stomach.

"My dad." Jun looked dazed. "He's dead. They killed him."

Her lip quivered and she stared into the distance, looking away from the corner of the room where her father lay crumpled. His neck twisted at an unnatural angle.

Nikolai held her, and after a moment, she pressed closer to him.

Sirens wailed in the background. Nikolai heard the echoing thud of something collapsing.

Jun sniffled, and Nikolai held her tighter.

26

Jun frowned at the shadows as she surveyed her roommate. "We can't leave her like this."

Suzie paced the dorm room, eyes blackened and drool running down her mouth. Teeth snarling.

The black rabbit gave her a disgruntled look.

"Look, I know she's an asshole, but I still can't leave her like this."

The rabbit pretended that it couldn't hear her and hopped onto Jun's bed, settling down on the covers. She was more moody than the white rabbit.

"Can we change her back, just for now? We can always do this" —Jun gestured at her hissing roommate— "again. If we need to."

The black rabbit cocked an ear up at this and put a paw to the chin, considering. Finally, slowly nodding. She thumped her hind leg against the covers and the sound rang, echoing out. Heavy.

Suzie stopped pacing and rubbed both palms against her eyes.

"Uhh, are you okay?" Jun stepped closer tentatively. One

hand reached back toward the rabbit in case Suzie tried anything.

"What are you talking about? Why wouldn't I be okay?" Suzie glared at her with her usual disdain.

Oh, good. She was back to normal. Cornea white, instead of a demonic void and everything.

"Umm, don't you have a final now?" Jun asked.

"What are you talking about? My math final isn't until the morning."

"Yeah, you might want to check your phone."

Suzie muttered under her breath. Something, something, Jun's a pain. Something like that as she pulled out her phone. She froze as she looked at the date and time across the screen. "What the hell! How is it morning already?"

"Yup," Jun said.

"Shit!" Suzie stuffed her manicured fingers into her mouth. "I didn't even study. I was supposed to study last night."

"Yeah, you've been out of it all night."

"My final started five minutes ago!"

"Maybe you should hurry, then," Jun suggested.

Suzie didn't even stop to say something rude. Just grabbed her backpack and rushed out the door.

"All right," Jun said to the dark rabbit who had snuggled into the covers. "That went well. I guess."

Jun sighed and put on the neon red and blue of her Feelin' Saucy uniform. For her last shift. The end of an era of cheap pizza. She'd have to say goodbye to her employee food discount.

Jun walked the path to her college cafeteria, but it was different now. Maybe because it was the last time. Maybe it was all of the yellow police tape cordoning off buildings damaged by the earthquake.

Jun shook her head. She didn't have time to think about the earthquake right now.

"Hey," Jun said to Alexa at the register.

"Hey, yourself. Ready to be free of this place?"

"Don't you know it," Jun replied, grabbing the key to the Crust.

"So, whatever happened to that hot guy following you around?" Alexa asked before Jun could step around the back.

"Oh, him." Nothing much. He'd just killed some of his teammates for her. And stopped her from going on a massive killing spree. "Uhh. He kissed me. So I guess that means he doesn't hate me."

"O-M-G! Are you guys, like, dating?"

"No. It was kind of a heat of the moment thing. During the earthquake."

"We can work with that. When are you going to see him again?"

"I don't know."

"Oh, my God! Jun! Go get your man."

"It's not like that."

"Sure, Jun. You keep telling yourself that." Alexa laughed.

Her last shift went quick. She had to get creative with her driving, as multiple intersections were still undergoing construction and repair. But she got the deliveries out without incident. When she went to return the keys, Alexa was already off her shift. So that was that. No more inquiries into Jun's love life. Or lack thereof.

Plenty of time for Jun to change out of her uniform. And get to her Business Analytics class early for the final exam.

Jun slipped into the back row of the auditorium. Silently observing her classmates that filed in. And the ones that didn't come in. Jun slipped further down in her seat and held her head in her hand.

Rick was studious and dependable. Definitely in the top of her class.

Tom. She had never spoken to Tom. But he seemed like a nice guy. He was always hanging around his clique, always talking about the next Comic-Con or something in his fandom.

Evan. A bit immature. Not the best student. Totally innocent.

None of them deserved to die.

Then there was Bailey. She'd texted him earlier, after she heard word that he was out of the coma. He was okay, considering. They were going to let him make up the final sometime next week.

This is your fault. Jun shook her head. She'd never asked for any of this to happen.

Nikolai walked in. He strode up the stairs to the back row, nodding to Jun as he passed her down the aisle. Plopping himself down three seats away. What was he doing here?

He wasn't still suspicious of her? Was he?

At the back of the auditorium, at precisely 8 p.m., Professor Cartwright came in. He was in a wheelchair. Grumpier than Jun had ever seen him, with their finals stacked up in his lap. Jun was out of the loop. She hadn't even heard any rumors that he might be getting out of the hospital soon.

He surveyed the class, which fell silent at the sight of him.

What was he going to say? Updates on his condition? Could he be happy to be back? Did he hear about the kids missing from his class?

"I see that none of you are getting the extra credit." Cartwright sniffed.

Oh, right. That. The suits and ties—Cartwright's sexist extra credit policy. Jun wouldn't have qualified anyway, even if she had come to class in a formal suit and tie. Cartwright had stared blankly at her when she had asked.

With that warm welcome, his teaching assistants started to walk up and down the rows, passing out the exams.

The white rabbit hopped out of her bear bag as Jun took out her pencil. He hopped around her head and did some cartwheels around her desk to cheer her up.

She smiled at his antics, brushing soft fur in-between questions.

Nothing but a hundred and twenty multiple choice questions stood between her and graduation.

Jun read a question and marked it with a C. With none of her usual anxiety.

On to the next. One of those trick questions that Cartwright was so fond of. The type one had to read a couple of times to figure out which answer was the best. Jun remembered this one from her notes. She marked the answer booklet with an A.

She didn't bother with circling answers in her test booklet that she was less confident about to tally and keep tabs on her potential score. She didn't fuss with annotating test questions and reading through them two to three times. Jun just answered the questions.

This test was the last thing she needed for her degree.

So why did she feel like it didn't matter anymore?

Jun finished and waited until a few others turned theirs in. She dropped her test off in the pile and walked out of the room. Done.

Jun drifted off to a familiar looking bench and sat, her head in her hands. Staring at the grass.

She hadn't noticed that Nikolai had followed her until he sat down next to her on the bench. She managed a small smile in greeting.

"What's wrong?" Nikolai asked.

Jun shook her head. "It's stupid."

"It's not stupid if it's upsetting you."

Jun rubbed her wrist, remembering her dad taking her out to eat to commemorate her second-place win in the spelling bee. How he grinned as he held her hand, guiding her across the street.

"My dad and I were supposed to celebrate. We were going to go to The Sushi Blanket." Now that was never going to happen.

Nikolai stood and held his hand out to her. "Come on."

"What?" Jun took his hand and let Nikolai pull her to her feet. His hand lingered, his thumb stroking slowly across her palm. He was warm. Energy flickered where his skin touched hers.

Her heart beat faster.

"Let's go. You're supposed to be celebrating."

"You don't have to do that." Jun frowned.

"You're still graduating. And I probably should get around to trying fancy uncooked fish."

"Wait, what? You've really never eaten sushi?"

Which was how Jun found herself at the best sushi restaurant in town, with her good friend the assassin.

"That one's salmon. That's a classic." Jun motioned to the plate of Alaska roll as it drifted by flirtatiously on a conveyor belt. Nikolai scooped it up and added it to his growing collection.

"The one after that is good, too." Jun pointed to the baked lobster roll, which ended up in Nikolai's sushi horde.

"That one's my favorite." Jun pointed out the rainbow roll. Nikolai plucked the plate up, sliding it in front of Jun. "Thanks."

For the next few minutes, Jun was lost in food heaven. The salmon was so smooth. She got the perfect bite, paired with creamy avocado. With just enough salt from the soy sauce. Perfect. Nikolai dropped whole rolls in his mouth they were popcorn. Which probably meant that he liked it. Or still thought he was starving from his self-imposed diet.

"What I want to know" —Nikolai gestured with his chopsticks, roll and all, with considerable dexterity for someone who'd never eaten with wooden sticks before— "is how you set off a magnitude nine-point-one earthquake for seven minutes. With no casualties."

"Hey, I was mad, all right? But I didn't want anyone to die."

"And no tsunami. Researchers are going to dedicate their lives to figure that one out."

"Oh, right. I forgot about tsunamis."

Nikolai chuckled. "So you're telling me no one died because you didn't want them to?"

"Well, yeah."

"You always manage to surprise me." Nikolai watched her, pale eyes intense.

Heat flooded her cheeks, and Jun looked away, fiddling with a bit of ginger on her tray. "So what are your plans now? Are you going to go kill some more bad guys?"

Nikolai shook his head. "I'm retiring."

Oh.

"Where are you going to go now?"

"I don't know. But I'm starting to like it around here," Nikolai said, looking right at her.

Jun bit her lip. *He definitely doesn't hate me.*

At their end of the meal, they got back the check on a tray with two fortune cookies.

Damn. A cookie would be the perfect thing to top off dinner. But wasn't a fortune what started this whole mess?

"I probably shouldn't open those." Jun frowned at the cookie.

Nikolai pointed to the one on the left. "That one is light, if it makes any difference."

"It's probably fine." Jun snapped the fortune cookie open. She read the fortune and grinned. "It says, 'Open up a craft store.'"

Her life-long dream of her own store was meant to be— foretold by prophecy and everything. *Perfect.*

Nikolai took the other, cracking it open and tossing the pieces into his mouth. He glanced down at the paper and swore so loud that other diners looked over at them.

Jun leaned in to catch a glimpse of his fortune.

Protect the magician. Others come to kill her in three months.

THANK YOU FOR READING!

If you enjoyed reading, please leave a review! Honest reviews help bring the book to the attention of other readers.

ACKNOWLEDGMENTS

So much love and support goes into writing a book.

Thank you Sierra Smith for your wonderful editing! This book is so much better because of your thoughtful suggestions.

I'd also like to thank all of my critique partners and especially AV Asher and Phil. Thank you for pointing out when I wrote things that made sense in my head, but not to anyone else.

Thank you Robynne and Damon at Damonza for the cover. Your work is stunning.

Most of all I would like to thank my friends and family. I love you all.

ABOUT THE AUTHOR

Renée des Lauriers is the author of the Divination in Darkness series. Renée was raised by a folk-singer and an accountant to be analytically creative. From thirteen, she played guitar and sang on stage at coffee shops. She also oil painted and wrote poetry on odd paper scraps. Besides writing, Renee has worked as an emergency medical technician and a high school English teacher. Now she lives in California with her family. Visit Renée online at www.reneedeslauriers.com.